Of Dreams and Drums

A novel by

Araby Patch

MEDUSA
PUBLISHER

MANHATTAN BEACH, CALIFORNIA
2010

PUBLISHED BY MEDUSA PUBLISHER

Published in the United States by
Medusa Publisher.

Library of Congress Cataloging-in-Publication Data
Patch, Araby
Of Drums and Dreams / Araby Patch
— 1st American ed.

ISBN 978-0-9827142-0-1

Printed in the United States of America

*Dedicated to those who seek
the sound of their own drums.*

CHAPTER 1

The junkie was coming back, doing his best to walk a straight line across the project grounds. He couldn't have been gone more than five minutes, thought Julio. It was too quick, and just too bad.

Somehow, the junkie's slippery eyes held onto Julio the whole way across. He stumbled through the playground, his body disjointed, alien like. He'd been a big man once, Julio could see, but now he was near wasting beyond the point where any reasonable man could come back.

The junkie jerked one way to miss a running boy and knocked a little girl to the ground. He didn't even look back; his eyes were pinned to Julio.

The little girl's mother jumped off her bench and shouted out, ready to pay this punk some mind, but Julio waved her off. She checked up her charge, but her mouth kept running. This guy was Julio's problem, he knew that. Everyone knew it. You could see it in his wild eyes—for the Junkie, there was nothing going on outside of Julio and what he held.

Julio readied himself. The junkie was still bigger than him, and a man. Julio was only just 18, and though he was athletic and a good fighter, he was still not yet a full-grown man. He'd have to take the junkie into the stairwell, hurt him quick, and hurt him good. There was no other way, and Julio hated it.

The junkie came up close. Julio could see the dried fluids white and flaky in the corners of his eyes and mouth. He was ready for the junkie's anger at the fake drugs he'd just sold him. He was ready for the attack. Just don't let it start out here, thought Julio. Just let me get him into the stairwell. Then there would be no witnesses and no cops, and Julio could put this guy down for a long time so he'd never come back.

"Yo, you got any more of that stuff?" said the junkie.

Julio couldn't believe it.

"Say what?" he said.

"You heard me, kid. That stuff got me right, now gimmie one more."

Julio couldn't tell if the man was serious or joking. There was no way to tell. Not yet. But Julio wanted to get him out of sight in the worst way.

"I got you, son," said Julio, "come on."

Julio began to walk, leading the junkie towards the stairwell. Not five minutes ago he'd sold the junkie half a crushed up Alka-Seltzer. He had two more baggies of it in his pocket. Everyone knew he didn't sell crack. He just sold weed, and even then only a couple of times. But this had been too tempting, too easy, he only did it to make the little extra cash he needed right now.

The worst part was Julio didn't plan on being out on the block for more than twenty minutes. This damn junkie came up first and came back too quick. Everything was going wrong. Nobody with a brain would carry real crack to a sale. The junkie was out of his mind.

Julio held the door and the junkie stepped in. The stairwell was a tiny, dark concrete room at the bottom of a steep steel staircase. It smelled like urine and the corners were stained darker than the shadows.

The door slammed shut closing the two of them in near darkness.

Julio readied himself for the beat down.

"You want one or two?" he asked.

In the dim light Julio could just see the junkie shooting glances from him to the door while he worked his jaw. His movements were quick and Julio could see now that he had a lot more bulk to him than he showed walking across the playground. It didn't seem like such a good idea to have this guy alone in the stairwell, but it was too late to turn back now. The junkie paused a moment longer, then his hand went quick into his pocket.

Julio brought up his fists, ready to knock away the gun or knife.

"Got ten bucks," said the Junkie. He held out a dirty wad of bills.

Julio put his hands down and took a deep breath.

"Come on kid, I don't got all damn day."

Julio smiled. "It's your lucky day, son. I got a sale going on."

Julio took the money and handed the man both the crushed up Alka-Seltzer baggies. He took them and examined the little baggies. Julio waited nervously.

The man looked doubtful, "You sure this the same stuff?"

Julio stiffened up.

"What did you say!?" he shouted. His words echoed up the stairwell. "I give you a deal and you gonna stand there testing me? I don't need you! Gimme my stuff back!" Julio threw the money at the man. It hit him in the face and fell at their feet.

The junkie didn't even look at the money. He just stared at Julio and Julio could see the pride well up in the junkie's face, he saw it come up and demand that he defend himself, he saw the fires of rage and disgrace come and just like on every other junkie he'd ever met, he watched as the little fragile baggies in the man's hands extinguish everything. In that instance, Julio knew he had the man beat.

"Pick up my money, crackhead!" shouted Julio.

The junkie picked up the cash and handed it to Julio. He hesitated a second, maybe to say something, maybe just to remember, and then he ran out the door and disappeared.

The door to the stairwell slammed shut and Julio was alone. He could hear his heart in the small of the stairwell. He tried to smile and tell himself how funny that was and he tried to feel pride about how he'd just handled the junkie, but deep down he felt sick of himself and sick of the lies.

Rage rose up in Julio. He squashed the weak feelings and pulled out the cash in his pocket and started to count it. He thought about how the money would get him what he wanted. He tried to smile.

Then he smelled the piss.

Julio kicked the door of the stairwell open and it slammed against the wall outside and came back. He kicked it again with everything he had.

It was a sunny, beautiful spring day in East Harlem and Julio felt like hell.

CHAPTER 2

Alone in his room, Julio took his time getting set for school. It was still early; he could tell by the sound of his aunt working in the kitchen. Julio caringly raised one of the brand new sneakers from a nest of packaging and admired it, turning it gently over and again in the early morning light, as if at any moment a genie might pop out to grant him unlimited wishes.

The shoes were immaculate, colored white with a blue gradient trim that spanned the temperature of the sky. The lines were aggressive and stylized and the soles unlike anything he'd ever seen. The leather slipped butter smooth under his fingertips as he traced the shape of the shoe, like the supple skin of lush feminine lips that would kiss his feet with every step.

He turned the shoe over again. They were the latest, most sought after style, so fresh off the rack that only a choice few on the block even knew they existed. They had cost him everything he had.

At School, he'd be the first to walk the halls sporting this particular style. A big smile came to his face. Pride filled him.

He pulled the laces free and reset them to street spec, then slipped them on one by one for the first time. He stood holding his pant legs up in front of the mirror so that he could see them clearly. They're perfect, he thought to himself. He sat back on the bed and with the softest of hands returned them to their protective plastic baggies then he slid them into his empty book-bag and pulled the drawstring closed.

Like a bad dream, images of that junkie came to his head. The sick feeling came up in him again and he pushed it away and thought again about the shoes and Maria Mary Sanchez with her fine body and big liquid eyes that made his heart skip a beat every time she looked at him. He thought about how she would be so impressed with him and his new shoes.

There was no denying his ability to make cash now. And forget about his fine taste and fresh style—it was indisputable. She would have to forgive him and give him a second chance once she saw how he'd changed and made something of himself.

He put on his humble old sneakers, the ones with the worn out soles and crunchy dry leather and then he went out.

In the kitchen, he met his three cousins Mariela, Monica and Miguel eating breakfast. Mariela was the oldest and on her way to being as beautiful and headstrong as her mother. She just ignored Julio when he came in.

Monica was younger, but almost to that age where she would start ignoring Julio too. She waved hello with her loose hand and spying her older sister's inaction, quickly went back to eating with a blank, impersonal stare.

Miguel was the youngest. He looked up and with a mouth full of cereal and yelled, "Juuuuuuliooooo," while little bits of cereal and milk dribbled down his chin.

Mariela turned red and shot him a look.

"You talk with your mouth open again and I'll close it for good," she snapped, turning on Miguel and raising her hand to prove it.

Miguel shut his mouth, but he kept the smile, eating away in silence.

"What's up," said Julio, grabbing some toast off the table on his way to the door.

"You aint even gonna eat?" demanded Mariela.

Her contempt for Julio flooded the small kitchen space. It was the tone she always took when speaking to him. Julio stopped with the door open, his bag on his back, and took a big bite of the toast.

"I didn't realize you cared so much," he said, allowing a curt smile before letting go the door.

Down the hallway halls with the musty painted walls and the creaky floors Julio came again to the stairs as he did every morning.

But, this time was different. He peeked back to make sure nobody was following him then sat down on the top step and took out the new shoes. Just the sight of them brought back the big smile. They were light as little feather pillows. When he slipped them on, he felt that cool, soft, new shoe feel. He stuffed the old sneakers in his book bag, stood, and dusted off, then descended into his first morning with the new shoes leading the way.

On the street, he walked with his eyes down, watching the tips of his new sneakers as they bounced before him. When he looked up he became conscious of the eyes of those who passed by. Like the boy hosing down the sidewalk in front of the building. He stared as Julio passed. The shoes practically glowed in the sunlight as he turned the corner. He passed a group of younger boys on the corner and they didn't even bother looking up at Julio's face, but rather looked down at his shoes.

"Damn!!" one of them exclaimed, "Check them fresh kicks out!"

Julio felt his head fill with pride and quickened his step towards the train. The shoes were unstoppable! Maria couldn't say no to him now. There was no denying his superstar status. He felt his walk hit stride. His shoulders dipped and swayed back and forth like the horns of a bull. Pride flowed in his veins for the first time in a long while, pride for himself, pride for his choices, pride for his manhood, and feeling that pride, knew he belonged. He knew he was on the rise.

At the 116th street station, with his shoes leading the way, a thought came into his mind. He spotted the bodega by the subway stop. Just outside the doorway sat a bucket of roses unguarded in the doorway. Julio looked around, and even though the streets were filling with people, it didn't look like anyone was watching. So he strode up casually towards the subway stairs, and quick as a cat snatched a rose from the bucket.

The response was almost instantaneous. "Hey, you! Damn kid!" Came the shout from inside the store, but Julio, with a single squeak of his new shoes, disappeared down the subway stairs before the owner of the bodega came running out.

The owner was going to run after him, but an old man on the street stepped in his way.

"It's o.k., Felipe. Relax," said the old man, "Todo chévere, amigo, I buy the rose for the kid. How much do I owe you, brother?"

Felipe stood and stared in disbelief. He tried to see past and find the kid, but the old man stood in his way. He looked at the old man, whom he'd know for over thirty years, as if he were a complete stranger.

"The boy's in love, amigo. Nada más, nada menos."

"What you talking about?" demanded Felipe, "You crazy, Viejo. That kid stole the rosa. I saw him."

But the old man just smiled. "How much, Felipe? How much for one of your precious rosas?"

"That kid no good, Rafa, you making a mistake." But the owner could see the old man wasn't going to heed. Finally Felipe relented, yelling at the old man, "You want to pay? Fine, you pay – one dollar!"

Rafael Alonso y Pacheco smiled, took a dollar from the hat he had placed on the sidewalk only moments before, and gave it to the owner.

As the owner went away shaking his head, Rafael went back to work setting up his drums. He whistled lightly as he placed the pair of ancient congas into position in front of his trusty old stool. The drums were old, older than he it seemed, but their sound was true to the way of the ancestors and when he played them something inside of the people awoke, something that had long been forgotten, and something that was welcome in their hearts anytime.

When he finished setting up he began to play a light jostling rhythm that was more a warm up than anything else.

A million mental miles away, Julio emerged holding the stolen rose on 103rd street. At the top of the steps he checked himself in the reflection of a shop window. He smiled at the new sneakers and walked on. He could feel the people and their jealously towards his new shoes, and in that feeling he felt himself rise above them, so that it was as if he were looking down from a high place over their pathetic, shoeless lives. He told himself that he was better than everyone. He was the one with the shoes, and in his mind he told each and every one of them to back up out of his way.

Julio pulled his hat down, dragging a dark shadow over his eyes. Feelings of power and mystery flared up around him like the licking flames of a hungry fire. The rose seemed almost too feminine in his hand. It was a blemish on his new tough guy image that was at this very moment emerging. So he stopped, and with little care stuffed the rose in his bag with his broken old shoes.

With his hands newly freed, he allowed them to swing in daunting form so that as he walked down the street, people parted the way for him to pass.

Arriving at school, he walked past the security guard.

"Take off your hat."

"Ya, ya, papi," said Julio, "I got you."

The security guard shook his head and went back to his daily paper.

Julio walked as he always did, into the bathroom where he took his hat off and checked his hair in the mirror. Everything looked good, just as it should. With his hat off and the shoes unseen, he looked into the mirror where Julio's eyes met with his own. In them he saw someone he didn't recognize and this new element of his personality both frightened and invigorated him at the same time. The new Julio didn't care about what people thought of him, it didn't want to please people anymore, it was about getting his while he could.

About doing me, he thought. He wasn't going to let anyone stand in his way, not now, not ever again. The new Julio wasn't a poor Spanish kid from the ghetto. He was somebody—somebody to be feared. He didn't care that he'd lost his mother to drugs in the streets, he didn't care because not only was he from the streets, he was the streets. And on the streets, sometimes you pay. My mother paid, and before I pay, I'm gonna get paid, he thought. He was going to do it his way, or die trying, he concluded.

Julio spotted some hesitation in his eyes, but before he could investigate he turned, grabbed his bag and headed back out into the hallway.

The classroom door opened easily. There were fifteen others seated in their desk chairs watching the teacher and every eye turned when Julio came in. He saw the words 'GED Science' scratched in chalk on the board. Near the front he spotted a student with his finger pressed into the pages of an open book. He must have been reading just before Julio came in.

"Well, Julio. Long time, no see," said the teacher, and he checked his watch just to make a point, "As usual—you're late."

Julio smiled sheepishly, and seeing Maria, gave her a little nod. She rolled her eyes in return.

"Sorry Mr. Cooper, but I had some things to take care of."

Mr. Cooper wasn't impressed, "Please find your seat, Julio. Lonnie, continue reading where you left off."

And so Lonnie's eyes found his held finger and he began again to read from his seat in the front of the classroom as Julio found his way to a seat in the back. As he walked he scanned his peer's faces for the recognition and jealousy he knew was sure to come when they spotted his new shoes.

At break, Julio found Maria Mary Sanchez where she always was, down the very end of the hall near the candy machine with her friends, Latisha and Coco. The girls liked to hang out there, near the exit door where they could sneak out for a smoke when nobody was watching. Julio came up on them and took the rose out of his bag. It was broken in the middle, but he didn't notice until it was too late. The girls all snickered.

Julio hesitated.

"Can I talk to you," he said, with no place to go.

"Go ahead," she said, and the other girls laughed.

"Can we go outside?" he pointed at the door.

"You can go wherever you want. But, *we* going nowhere," she said, pointing at Julio and herself.

Julio felt his blood rising in a hot flash, but he held it down and tried to play it cool.

"Come on, Maria, don't be like that. Let's go outside a minute."

"What, you too good to talk to me in front of my friends now that you got some dumb-ass new shoes and a busted-ass flower?" she shook her finger at his shoes and his flower.

Julio stood silently, holding the broken flower.

"You think you all hot now cause you got a couple coins, got youself some new sneakers, you think you all that?" She scoffed, "Well, let me tell you, you aint nothing! You still in a GED school," Maria said.

"Barely," Coco chimed in.

"And, you still live with your aunt," Maria continued.

"You aint no real man," said Latisha.

"You all better shut up," he warned.

"Or what," said Maria, she was getting angry now. Her face was pinched tight, "What? What you gonna do?"

Julio just stood there.

"Look at you, trying to be all hard or somethin," said Coco.

"Let me tell you something, Julio. We had something—till you messed it up." Maria took a breath trying to cool down. She looked him up and down, "What happened to you?" she asked. "You think you can impress me with some sneakers?" she looked for his eyes, but they were on the ground now, "You aint no man." she concluded.

"He barely even a boy." Said Coco, just before her and Latisha burst out laughing. They slapped five, facing each other.

The rage flared, blinding Julio. He stepped up and in a flash slapped Coco square in the eye as hard as he could. He'd come in real quick, just like always. Maria was the only one who saw it coming. She jumped forward trying to shove him away, but she was too late. As Coco spun back from the slap, Maria followed up with a full-fisted swing at him, but he easily blocked it just as Latisha swung from the other side and glanced his shoulder with a harmless punch.

Julio bounced back, unhurt, at the ready and safely out of the way as Coco came at him with all-out wild eyes. Maria stepped in front of her and held her back and the whole thing brought a twisted smile to Julio's face.

"I'll kill you, I swear! Nobody hits me! I'll kill you!" Coco was screaming at the top of her lungs, her voice filling the hallways and her arms and elbows ripping wild in a fight for freedom from Maria's grasp.

"Chill coco!" Maria yelled into her face, "Chill! He aint worth it!"

She had to hold Coco tight and if it hadn't been for Latisha coming in, Coco would have easily broken free of Maria's hold.

"Chill!" shouted Latisha, when she got a good grip, "He aint nothing but a punk! It aint worth it! Let it go!"

Coco cooled out a second, she touched her eye, which was beginning to swell, "Damn!" she shouted, "Punk-ass! I'll kill you! I ever see you again and you dead!"

"Get outta here!" demanded Latisha.

"You watch. I'll kill you, Julio," said Coco.

"Ya, you try it, and you'll see what you get," said Julio, and he tossed the rose down toward the exit door.

Julio snatched up his bag and walked—past his teacher Mr. Cooper, past the security guard and out the big doors at the front of the school.

On the street he headed for the train with his hat pulled low and his blood boiling.

When he came up at 116th, the old man Rafael was there playing his drums. Rafael watched Julio come up the steps and saw the anger on him. Julio was walking as if he were on his way to kill someone and to this Rafael shook his head slowly to the rhythms that poured like water from his hands. Julio passed by, not five feet from Rafael's drums, and didn't look up even once. Rafael watched him go while he held the rhythm in his hands.

A woman passed and dropped a few coins into the hat. Rafael turned and smiled.

"You the best, papi," she said and began to dance a bit in front of him.

Rafael laughed and with a quick soloing flurry came to a lively salsa groove that sent the woman spinning joyfully down the street. He followed her with his smile until she turned the corner, and then his smile faded away and his play slowed and calmed as he searched down the block for Julio.

But Julio was gone; disappeared into the hustle and heat of 116th in the early afternoon.

CHAPTER 3

Julio couldn't believe Maria had shunned him like that. Didn't she know who he was, who he would be. Not a man? She didn't know what she was talking about. He was gonna be the best man on the block. He would show her, he thought. I'm gonna be the baddest, most feared man the barrio has ever seen. Then I'll go find her and her pathetic friends and won't even spend twenty seconds of my precious time laughing at her sorry ass. Then, I'll forget her forever. Even if she called him every minute, he would just ignore her, he decided.

Beside him on the street a brand new BMW M5 rolled up, cruising with the sounds of bass low and smooth bumping from the lowered windows. It was Santos, the undisputed, biggest, baddest gangster in the barrio, and he had two girls in the car with him, both beautiful and dressed to kill. Santos crawled by in his BMW and saw Julio standing there staring as he passed. With the stereo smoothing the air, the girls laughing and hanging off his right arm, and a knowing smile spreading across his face, Santos gave a little nod to Julio as he passed—cool as could be.

Julio could only watch them go by. Santos revved the engine and in an instant they were gone.

Like that! He said to himself, I'm gonna get mine, just like Santos. "Damn," he whispered under his breath, "look at them girls." And they were beautiful, more beautiful than Maria even, and he could tell they knew how to pick a man—not like Maria. Maria didn't know nothing! In Julio's mind, he saw himself driving through the streets behind the wheel of his new car with the girls hanging off of him. Just like Santos, but better. Julio would travel with three girls, not two, and they'd all call him Papi, and if one of them got jealous of the other, he'd throw her out and get a new one. Julio could see the images clearly as they filled his head. Chased by a sly smile, Julio flew up the steps of his building and into the small apartment where he lived with his aunt.

He opened the door, dancing on the dreams of what would be. Then with a flare, kicked the door shut behind him. It slammed, causing his aunt Sylvia to jump and spill her coffee wide across the table where she'd been sitting quietly beneath the long shadows of the kitchen.

"Julio, pero qué haces!?" she shouted, rising to wipe up the newly spilled coffee before it ran off the table and onto the floor.

"Sorry tía, I didn't know you were home." Julio said, "Why aren't you at work?" he added.

"Why aren't you at school?" She stopped cleaning and looked up at him.

Julio began taking his bag off. His eyes were all over the room.

"There was no teacher today," he lied, and then put his bag down. "They sent us home."

His aunt's face pinched tight.

"You gonna lie to me?"

Julio moved sheepishly towards a chair at the table as Sylvia stared at him, her eyes filling with fire.

"No tia, I won't lie," he said finally, "the truth is, I just left. Maria made me mad, so I left.

"Oh," said Sylvia, then with gathering distance the name harmlessly floated away, "Maria."

At that she turned and began making another cup of coffee. Julio waited for her to berate him for skipping class, he waited for the shouts and curses that always came, he waited for her to scream about how his mother would be so upset if she could see him, he waited for her to throw things in the small kitchen and perhaps even to slap him, but she just poured herself another coffee, added the boiled milk from the stove and some sugar from the cup on the counter, and stirring it with a spoon, sat back down. Sylvia sighed and stared into the cup of coffee. Julio could see her shoulders were heavy and her mind was spinning.

"What's wrong, tia?" he asked.

She hesitated.

"I won't skip anymore, I promise." he said.

Her face pinched up at him again, but not as harsh as before, "Ya right."

"What's wrong, tia?" Julio asked again.

"Nada," she said, "there's nothing wrong," but he pressed, putting his hand on hers.

"Come on, tia. Tell me."

She sighed again, "I lost my job today," she said. "They said before that it might happen, I was praying that they wouldn't, I thought they wouldn't, but they laid off so many people." She moved her hand out from under Julio's. "So many people, Julio."

Julio sat back, his ears felt hot and there was a tingling across his neck and head.

"I don't know what we're going to do, Julio." She looked him in the eyes, "No way I can pay the rent this month. That's three in a row. No rent, and the landlord told me yesterday that if I don't pay we have to go." She looked at Julio a moment, and then got up abruptly to begin wiping down the counter.

Julio wanted to say something, but he didn't know what to say. He wished he could help her with the rent. He wanted to help her so badly. But there was nothing he could do. He stood and taking up his bag said, "Don't worry tia, everything will be o.k."

She turned, drying her hands with the towel and nodded her head, wishing as much as Julio had been that those words were true. But, when she saw Julio the faint smile she wore dropped to the floor with disappointment. Just as quick, her face lit up with anger and her mouth exploded with rage.

"What are you doing with those!?" she screamed, pointing at his shoes.

Julio had forgotten the shoes! He'd meant to take them off before she saw them. He'd meant to take them off downstairs, or in his room, he didn't know she would be there when he got home. She came up on him quick.

"Are you crazy?" she yelled and before Julio could think to move, she slapped him full in the face.

Julio spun and dropped his bag but she was too quick and slapped him again, this time in the ear and so hard he nearly fell over. He turned and with his back against the wall waited for her to come again. He wasn't going to let her hit him again. She came up, her hair wild now and her mouth jagged with tears and rage and she kicked as hard as she could and Julio raised his leg and blocked her. Then she came at him with both hands slapping, and grabbing her wrists he held her, the both of them struggling in the kitchen, moving across the floor knocking down a chair, then another and against the far wall and Sylvia still struggling and Julio struggling to hold her so that she could not hit him again.

"Calm down, tia!" he shouted. "Cálmate!"

She struggled for a moment more and then looked into his eyes with hatred then disappointment and finally disgust. She stepped back and sensing the fight gone out of her, Julio freed her arms. She went to the sink and grabbing the edges began to wail uncontrollably. Julio went about the kitchen in silence replacing the chairs and trying to return the space to normal. Sylvia put her head down on the edge of the sink and cried with everything she had.

Finding his bag, Julio picked it up and with a final glace at his aunt, her back rolling with sobs, her head down at the sink, he walked the hall to his room.

After a while she came knocking, "Where did you get the money for those shoes?" she demanded.

"I saved it."

She tried to contain herself, but her mouth was coming apart, "You lie to me again," she said, the words shaking on her lips, "and I will beat you and never stop."

Julio let his head drop. They both knew where he got the money, why did he have to say it?

"You keep your drugs out of my house," she said, "You hear me?"

"I would never-"

"You don't know what you do! Not anymore!" Sylvia interrupted him.

Julio couldn't look at her. He didn't mean to make her mad. He wanted to tell her that everything was o.k., but he knew it wasn't and he knew if he said the wrong thing she would beat him again and not stop and he was afraid of what he might do to defend himself.

"Your mother." She began again, "My sister. She hung on the block. With those drug dealers. Said they treated her nice, but I know better. They just used her. Used her until she was dried up and wasted. Then when there was nothing left, they took her life. All the time she chased dreams. She was a dream chaser, just like you Julio. Never did her dreams come true. Not until she had you. She thought you would save her. But you were just a baby, just like her. And nobody could save her. Not her dreams, not you, not me, not anybody." It was a story he'd heard a thousand times, and it was a sad story, but each time she told it he wanted to hear it and he wanted to hear more.

"I took you because I loved my sister. I took you from the streets, like my own. I have my babies and I have you." This was the part he didn't like, "Look at me," she said, but he couldn't. "Fine, you stare at the ground, because that's where you're going."

He looked up.

"You 18," she continued, "You drop out of school because of this, you sell drugs because of that, you go to GED school because I make you, and you don't do anything but chase crazy girls there, then you come home and you bring all your garbage from the street into my home. And, my babies are watching you." She was heating up again and her voice shook and wavered in a high, near breaking pitch, "You the only man in the house." The tears were coming now, "What kind of house do you want me to live in?"

Julio knew this part was about Sylvia's husband leaving her for another woman. He knew it because he'd been there and he'd seen the same look on her face when she yelled at him that day he left for good. But Julio also knew if he said one word, even one word about that day, Sylvia would loose all control. So he sat there, taking it.

"I called my cousin Mary, she say we can live with her for a while. I think I got to move out of here now. No job. No money." She stared hard at Julio now, "And you. Out there selling drugs and spending money on shoes while I bust my ass paying for your food and your bed." She wiped her face with her hand, the hand was shaking. "I'm taking my babies to my cousin's house. But she says there's no room for someone like you!"

"What?"

"No room! I said no room! You have to find a place to live. You 18. You a big man now, with your money and your new shoes. You know what's best for you." Her tongue was like a whip as she said it.

"Tia, you kicking me out?"

"About time, don't you think?" she said, still whipping him.

Julio didn't want this. His mind was reeling. He tried to catch a moment by holding his head between both hands. His eyes fell down to his busted old sneakers. He had an idea.

"I'll take them back." He said.

"What did you say?"

Julio raised his head, "I said, I'll take them back. I'll take the shoes back and you can use the money for rent."

"Huh," she scoffed, unimpressed.

But then the idea, like a cruel twisting weed, took root.

"OK, you take them back, and you give me the money for rent," she stepped up and pointed her finger, "And you going to get a job too, no more school, no more girls and no more drugs. You going legit, kid. You're going to help me pay for this place and you gonna become a man. Or you out! I see you slip once," she shook her head and sucked her teeth, "you out, Julio."

The demands were heavy and Julio knew it, but there was nothing he could do. At that moment he wanted everything his aunt did, he wanted to make her proud and he knew if he could help his aunt it would go a long way in repaying her for taking him off the streets after his mother died. He knew that he must do what she asked, yet he was afraid that he would fail.

"I'll do it tia, I'll become a man." He said finally.

She considered him a moment; calculating, calm.

"Yea, you will," she said finally, "You'll be a man—someday."

She rose and walked to the door, and then turned.

"I just wonder what kind of man you'll decide to be." She said, and she left him alone in his room.

CHAPTER 4

The next day, Julio ate at the table for the first time in a long while, silently chewing his food beside his cousins and aunt. He hadn't heard his aunt tell his cousins the story of their fight or her losing her job, but he knew they knew. All the world ate silently at the table, until Sylvia packed up and without a word walked out in search of a new job. The cousins, walking solemnly only seconds behind, also packed their things for school and without looking back left Julio alone in the kitchen.

He did the dishes for the first time in a long time and prepared to go downtown to take the shoes back.

When he got to his room, he took them out of their wrapper one more time. The leather was so smooth and soft, and the colors so fly, the soles like nothing he'd ever seen before. He held them up, tossing them lightly as a father would a newborn.

He marveled at their perfection. They were the most spectacular shoes he'd ever seen. Julio started to put them away again, but then he thought of how when he walked down the street the day before, everyone treated him with a new kind of respect. He thought about how powerful he felt walking with the new shoes on his feet and how that power had made him feel like a man. He slipped them on again, just one last time he told himself, and walked around the room. They looked good on his feet. So good! He felt the pride rising within him and his mind went to work.

You look good in these, it told him. You deserve to look good! Selling drugs wasn't the bad part, being stupid and wearing these into the house was. You can get paid. You a player, kid! All you need to do is wise up. Just wise up! Julio stood in his room with the voice ringing in his head.

Then a moment later, it was gone. He thought again of his promise to his aunt and decided right then and there he would take the shoes back and give her the money for the rent. That was the best thing for him to do, he knew this.

But, he could wear the shoes just one more day, on his way downtown to take them back. He'd rock them once more before he had to give them back. He deserved it. He grabbed his bag, stuffed the old shoes inside and went out.

Out on the street it was the same as before. He high stepped it down the block with all eyes upon him and his new shoes. He loved the attention, even more than the day before. The nervousness was fading and he could feel the jealousy rising around him, but he shook all that off and told himself he was the man. Coming around the corner, he almost slammed into Santos who walked alone in a super sleek sweat suit.

"Yo, look out kid," warned Santos.

"My bad," said Julio.

Santos was a big, good looking, light skinned Latino. A football player in high school, he'd only grown bigger, stronger and faster after dropping out to sell drugs. He'd killed off most of the other drug dealers in the area in sometimes brutal gangland style killings. Those that didn't die by his hand ran away to other, less dangerous neighborhoods. The fact that he'd survived so long was testament to his thorough planning and relentless dedication to the streets.

Respect for Santos ran deep and wide across the Puerto Ricans, the Mexicans and the African Americans. He ran the block, and everyone knew it. To see him walking, and to see him walking alone, was rare.

"Yo, hold up a second."

Julio stopped dead in his tracks. He turned.

"Whats up?" Julio asked.

"Yo, where you get them kicks?" asked Santos, "I gotta get me a pair of them."

"Downtown," said Julio.

"What they cost you?"

"Bout two fity," said Julio.

"Yea, that's what I though," said Santos and he took a good look at Julio. "I know you," he said, "you did a job for Tiny a couple weeks ago."

"Yea," said Julio, "that was me."

"He said you done real good," Santos eyed Julio up and down, until he decided something, "You want more work, you come find me, ya hear?"

"Yea?" asked Julio, "Cool."

Santos flashed his famous movie star smile, "I'm always looking for good soldiers like yourself, especially with a taste for the finer things in life," he nodded at the shoes.

"Word," said Julio.

"Word," said Santos.

They shook on it, and then Santos turned and walked on down the block.

Julio was beside himself.

Santos! Santos spoke to me! Asked me if I wanted to work for him! It was as if the angels were smiling upon him. Julio looked around with his head in the clouds. 'These shoes are the bomb!' he cried out in his mind.

Down the block, Rafa stood frozen in the midst of setting up his drums. He'd been watching Julio with the shopkeeper, Felipe, by his side. From his place, Rafa saw the whole exchange between Santos and Julio, and Rafa was all too aware of who Santos was.

Julio walked towards the entrance to the train. He knew the brief meeting with Santos was enough to step up his street game in a big way. Anybody who saw it would reconsider Julio's status. Santos didn't stop unless he knew it was something important, so that meant that Julio was important. The shoes were coming through! He didn't mind taking them back now, he knew in a few weeks he could buy six pairs if he wanted to, and his aunt's rent woes—a thing of the past. When he got up close to Rafa and the shopkeeper he couldn't take their stares any longer.

"You think you know me, old man?" Julio said, and spit on the sidewalk.

"You think you know you?" asked Rafa.

"What you say?" said Julio, stepping forward with his eyes hard in the face of Rafa.

But Rafa didn't flinch. His eyes were steady and calm and stared right back.

"Cuando el pato aprende a volar, ya no necesita andar," he said with no judgment.

"What?" said Julio sharply, "I don't be speakin no Spanish, old man."

Rafa was calm, and in cool tones replied, "When the duck learns to fly, he doesn't need to waddle anymore."

"Ha!" said Julio in a halted laugh, "You some kind of poet or something?"

"Learn Spanish, mijo, it's your culture," said Rafa.

"I got my culture right here, old man," said Julio and he grabbed his groin and broke out laughing.

Rafa grabbed his own groin and laughed right with him and just as hard and then even harder and Julio felt a sudden awkwardness in his laughing with the old man who Julio and his friends considered to be a no good bum on the streets, so he turned and began to walk off.

"You crazy old man, you crazy!" he said behind him.

Rafa watched him go.

Felipe shook his head. He looked to his old friend Rafa, a man he'd known for many, many years, a man he dearly respected and admired, "I told you, Rafa," he said, "that boy no good. No, no, no. He no good."

Rafael shook his head.

"No, Pana," he said, "no such thing as no good. Only those who know, and those who don't. He's just lost, papi, lost like the rest of them."

Felipe could only smile and shake his head at his optimistic old friend. Then he returned to the inside of his shop.

Rafael bent down and picked up his stool and set it before his drums. He set out the hat too, where those that did tossed coins to thank him for his daily playing. When all was set, he sat and immediately took up a rhythm that sounded like a warrior's dance.

Rafa's face was stern, his eyes staring into the nothingness before him as he played. The beats came quick, percussive, almost like guns going off in his hands. The rhythm was quick and steady as the feet of running warriors moving into battle with popping explosions on all sides. But the marching beats rolled on with no hesitation or fear, as if in the warrior's world death were not an end, but a doorway into another dimension. He held his unfocused gaze and the rhythms rolled on.

The sound of the drums rose up into the sky and filled the air. They came off the buildings and found their way down into the subway tunnel. But before they could reach Julio they fell away, lost in the echoes of the thundering train that blew through the hollow tunnel.

Julio looked around the subway car, lost in his mind, far away from where Rafa's drums could be heard. He looked around the subway car as it quietly rocked and clattered around him. One by one the people on the train passed through his gaze and to each and everyone he told himself he was better than they, until he'd counted off every person in the car.

When he was done with them he remembered the old man, Rafa. He'd made that old man look silly, he decided. The duck that learns to what? What did he say? It didn't even matter. Who was he calling a duck anyway?

He thought again of his meeting with Santos and dreams of cars and girls filled his head. He would get a gun too, just like Santos had. He'd seen the little bulge under Santos's arm on the street. He knew if he worked for Santos he would need one. Maybe Santos himself would give him one to use, a fine silver one with golden bullets, seeing as they both had similar taste in the finer things in life.

When the train stopped at 110th the doors opened and Julio went white. Coco and four guys stepped quickly into the car surrounding him with their hands in their pockets. The door slid shut and just before it closed Julio made a jump to get out but one of the boys blocked him with a shoulder.

"Aint your stop, son." Said the boy.

Julio was trapped. He'd never seen any of these boys before. He kicked himself. Why didn't I see them come up, he thought. What a fool!

Coco nodded to the biggest of the boys and he smiled at Julio. Coco's eye was still red from where he'd slapped her. She smiled, but hers was the smile of cruel irony. She blinked with the swollen eye, as if winking at Julio. He tried to walk down the car but there were two blocking that way.

"Let me through," demanded Julio.

"Nah, son, we got some business wich you," said the one with a toothpick in his mouth.

"Yea, we aint done here," said the one with the bad breath.

"Who is you?" asked Julio, "Takes four you punks to hold me down?" he turned back to Coco, "You all must be scared, you bitch."

"You the only scared bitch here, Julio," she said and smiled big.

The train slowed and came to a stop. Julio's mind was whirling as it looked for an escape. But the four had him dead trapped. They boxed him in and with sharp elbows and hands forced him out onto the platform. Julio just played it cool.

He knew better than to cause a scene. If he caused a scene they would beat and stomp him anyway and considering the job half done would hunt him down until they were through. Not to mention, to scream and cry and run would completely destroy his street reputation. No—they had him. He had to fight and fight his best or else they would never leave him alone.

So he prepared himself for the fight.

They were all at the end of the platform. The four boys spread out, blocking the way to the exit. Behind them, the platform was emptying and in a moment it would be clear, all except for the five of them and Julio. Coco stood in the middle with a big grin on her face.

"I bet you think twice before you slap a girl, again," she said.

"I bet he don't even look at a girl again after this," said the big kid.

Julio knew the big one was trouble. He was enjoying all this too much. He looked too comfortable, too ready, as if his days were filled with these types of confrontations—confrontations he rarely lost. Alone he could never take the big kid. The other three he knew he could take one-on-one, but this wasn't that kind of fight. If it were just the three he might be able to take them, if he fought right.

Julio instinctively took deep breaths and tried to calm his heart down.

Coco came around trying to get behind him, but Julio kept walking back. They were too many; he'd have to wait for his opening. He would have to wait for them to make a mistake. The big kid broke away and came up on the track side. He was popping his fist into his open hand and dancing on his feet, psyching himself up for the battle.

"I got you, son, I got you right here," he said, moving his way.

Then Julio saw his opportunity and took it. With all his quickness and strength he flew into the big kid, shoving him as hard as he could. The big kid steadied himself to take the charge but Julio's weight and strength surprised him, or perhaps he didn't realize where he was. Either way, the big kid flew off the platform and came crashing down sideways onto the tracks. Everyone heard the crack of his arm as it broke under him on the rail below. Coco came up quick and landed a punch right into Julio's ear. He turned and ducked her second and slipped the third and came up strong to meet the kid with the toothpick square in the jaw with an uppercut. The kid went down in slow motion, like in a dream, lucidly lit by the florescent flickering lights, and Julio saw the toothpick spinning in mid air and heard in his mind a voice yell, "Knockout!" and he actually had time in that suspended moment to feel pride.

In a flash, time resumed its normal course just as he felt a shoe drive up into his guts and felt all the air go out of him. He doubled over uncontrollably. The kid with the bad breath stepped up and as Julio bent over, unable to breath, the kid kicked him square in the face and Julio went over and down like a sack of boiled cassava. He turned and saw the third of the three smaller boys helping the big kid back onto the platform. He could just see the big kid's face over the platform edge. In that instant Julio registered the sum of the pain and sickness on the big kid's face; it was so white, almost green and there was a big cut over the eye that hadn't started bleeding yet and all the details of the big kid's injuries; the twisted arm and the face and the colorless skin, it all made him want to cry for the sorrow of it all.

But then, like a siren, he suddenly heard his own mind screaming for him to get off the ground, so he went up on one elbow just in time for Coco to kick him square in the groin with everything she had. Julio collapsed into a tight ball and felt another strong kick into his back just above his kidneys and another and still another then one more that spit his lips wide open. He tasted the blood and curled up as best he could, but the kicks rained down on him connecting with his head back and legs with countless concussions.

Then just as quick, the blows stopped.

Julio could barely move from all the pain. He heard someone scuffle over and felt the violence of his shoes being yanked off. He rolled over slowly and saw Coco holding the shoes. The kid with the toothpick was getting up with help from the kid with bad breath and behind he could see the last of them helping the big kid down the platform towards the exit.

"I should throw your ass onto the tracks," snapped Coco.

But Julio knew it was over. The taste for violence had been satisfied. Nobody wanted anymore. Except Coco, she wanted one more thing. She came over and tossed Julio's new shoes on the ground. She kicked him in the legs, hard.

"You ever put your hands on me again and I'll finish you," she said, and Julio didn't care.

He heard the train coming and saw Coco watching it come up from deep down the dark mouth of the tunnel. She licked her lips and Julio could see her turning things over in her mind.

"Tell me why I shouldn't just end you right now," she said and Julio saw in her eyes the wild anger capable of doing it.

He tried to move, but his muscles were either spasming uncontrollably or locked and swollen. He tried to roll over on his front to push himself up, but his face just pressed into the cold hard concrete. With a groan, he flopped over on his back again. Coco spit on him. He wanted to wipe it off, but his arms wouldn't move. The train was nearing. He could hear it coming fast with the wind pouring out the gaping tunnel in a singular billowing gust.

For a moment he caught her eyes with his. He held them, then felt himself go; she could do whatever she wanted—whatever, he didn't care. Coco let up, perhaps from pity, or fear, and stepped back, taking up his shoes again. She turned to spot the others and just as the train came screaming into the station she tossed the shoes under the braking wheels and walked off.

With great effort Julio brought himself to his knees. The train doors opened and the people poured out. Businessmen, students, mothers, fathers, kids with heavy bags and an old man with a creaky cane. They all went by on either side as Julio struggled alone and on his own to his feet. He stumbled and caught himself by grabbing a man dressed in a suit who walked by.

"Hey, back off, kid!" shouted the man and shook Julio off.

Julio found his balance and moved over to the wall and leaned back. The doors closed and the train rolled out. He looked down at his socked feet, then to the platform edge. Slowly he came over and peered down to the tracks. His shoes were gone.

He started walking in the direction of the train until he found one halfway down the platform. He could see it was badly damaged. Up the tracks it was silent; there was no sign of an oncoming train. Julio tested his strength before lowering himself down. Once on the tracks, he was surprised to find the platform came up to about his shoulder. Grabbing the shoe, he limped down the tracks. There were rats filing in and out of a hole under the platform edge. Julio tried to ignore them but they were big and unafraid. He stumbled on with half the platform to go and his socked feet collecting the grime of the subway tracks. He heard a few quick clicks coming from the rails and before he could take another step he heard the train coming up full speed behind him.

Julio turned and saw the lights of the train and heard the horn scream to life. It blew out the darkness of the tunnel opening and into the vague light of the station. He could see the conductor hammering the horn with his hand in the well-lit cockpit. Julio ran with his broken body away from the train with the one shoe in hand. Before him he saw the second shoe jammed beneath the outside rail, and with all his strength he bent down low at a full run and yanked, ripping it free. He ran hobbling and stumbling down the tracks until finally he'd outrun the train as it came to a screeching stop near the end of the platform.

Julio took the service steps at the end and doubled back, regaining the platform with shoes in hand. The conductor slammed his window open.

"What you trying to do, get yourself killed?"

But Julio just walked on.

"I'll call the police," the conductor continued, "You can't be on the tracks, I'll call the police!"

Julio ignored him and just walked away down the platform. When the train left, and the platform was clear, he surveyed the shoes. They were absolutely destroyed. Both had cuts in the leather and the once white elements looked to be permanently streaked with oil, grease and grime. The laces of one were severed and the other was missing half the tongue. That's what ripped free, he thought. No way they'll take these back now, he said to himself.

He looked for his bag down the platform. He looked for his bag with his trusty old sneakers, but it was gone. There was no choice. He put the broken shoes back on and was surprised to find that they still felt good on his feet. In fact, his feet never felt better. All he needed were some new laces.

He felt his lips and the side of his face where the first kick had landed. Everything was swollen and his fingers gingerly outlined the edges of at least two big cuts. The blood was thick and drying fast on his face. His kidneys were killing him. He limped down the platform and found his way to the uptown train heading home.

At the 116th street station Julio was surprised to see old man Rafa leaning over his drums, watching him come up the stairs to the sidewalk level, as if he'd been there waiting the whole time. Julio tried to straighten himself up, tried to find the pride he'd had going down, tried to keep the tears from coming.

The old man Rafa just watched him come.

"Well, at least you fight good," said Rafa just as Julio came even with him.

"Say what?"

"Look at it this way," said Rafa breaking a smile, "you still got your shoes."

Julio kept walking, "Screw you," he said, and Rafa broke into a hearty belly laugh that for all its richness didn't make Julio feel any better.

CHAPTER 5

When Julio got home, his aunt was in the kitchen at the table with the coffee again, staring into the cup as she stirred absently with the thin handle of the small spoon. When he came in this time there was no dancing, no kicking of the door.

It clicked shut behind him. He just wanted to get to his room. He didn't want to talk to her, didn't want to tell her about the shoes. He didn't want to explain anymore or make excuses anymore. He just wanted to lie down and go to sleep. He saw her and turned towards his room.

"Hey," she said, "you can't say hello?"

"Hello," he said and limped on.

"What happened to you?" she asked, rising.

"Nothing," he said and he was almost to his door now. He opened it and went in, going straight to the bed where he lied down.

She came to the doorway and looked in. He was on the bed, face down. His shirt dirty on the back with the dust of innumerable kicks. She saw the shoes, which he still wore, framed by the dark blue of the bedspread. She came forward, steadied by her outstretched hand as it slid down the wall by the bed.

"Jesus Maria y Jose, Julio," she said, her voice rising to treble, "What happened to you?" she rushed to his side hysterical, "What happened, Julio baby, what happened?"

She was touching him lightly on all his wounds in frantic despair. Touching his back where the kicks landed, the side of his face, touching him with quick, light fingers. She touched his hands that gripped the bedspread in a tight fist and looked down at the shoes in tatters on his feet.

"Oh, Julio," she wailed, "Oh, Julio," she cried.

And he couldn't hold it any longer, so he began to cry with all the pain of the fight and the sight of the big kid with his busted arm and green face. He cried for Maria Mary Sanchez and his mother and the shoes and the lost rent and his aunt who loved him and who cried at his side with him. He cried until he stopped and then she went out and he heard her in the kitchen. He listened to her and watched her movements with the images playing behind his eyes as she moved around the kitchen preparing a meal. He watched her in the darkness of his imagination until finally, he fell asleep.

When he awoke he came to his feet. The shoes were beside the bed in their broken splendor. He held his side as he walked down the hallway and knew that he'd be o.k. He knew that he'd gotten the better of them, even though they'd beaten him down. He knew that it was over for now between him and Coco and her friends. They had beaten him good, but he'd given them something to think about. At least they hadn't broken anything. He would be fine in a couple of days, and he still had his pride. That much was true.

Sylvia was working in the kitchen when he came in.

She didn't wait a second before laying into him.

"So, what did you do?" she asked. All the sugar was out of her voice now. "I see you still have the shoes."

"They're destroyed," he said.

"I saw."

She waited, but not for long.

"So. What happened? Why did you get into a fight?"

Her hands went tight against her waist.

"I got jumped," he said.

He didn't want to have this conversation now, not ever.

"Can we talk about this later?" he asked.

"No, we can't talk about this later."

She was all over the kitchen lifting this and moving that.

"What happened? Why did they jump you? Was it drugs? Are you in trouble with drugs?"

"No," he said. He felt so tired. "They just jumped me."

She stopped a moment to look at him, her foot tapping the floor, "For nothing?! Just for being you!? And who's they? Who they?" she asked.

"Just some people. I don't know."

Julio touched the side of his face and winced.

"And the shoes? Why didn't you take them back? What are we going to do now?" and her voice broke.

"The shoes?" he asked, his voice rising, "I was taking them back, they jumped me and threw the shoes on the tracks."

"Ya, right," she mocked, "they threw them on the tracks."

She spun to face him at the sink and he couldn't take it anymore.

"What are you talking about?" he said, and felt his face go red. "Did you see the shoes?! Look at my face, tia!"

She just stared at him, unmoved.

"They jumped me! They kicked my ass and took my shoes and threw them on the tracks!"

She wanted to strangle him.

"You're so full of lies!" Her words flew at him like knives, "You're nothing but a no good liar!"

She was screaming now.

"Liar!" she screamed, "Liar!"

"Aaaaaahhhhh!!!" Julio yelled and jumped up. His chair flew back against the wall and with profound strength he took the edge of the table in his hands and lifted it toy like, flinging it across the kitchen. It barely missed knocking Sylvia to the ground.

She stood back horrified with her heart in her hands. The table rattled amongst the debris it created in falling as Julio stood, his chest heaving with breath, his face red and dampened by sweat, his wild eyes only now finding the present and what had just transpired. He looked at Sylvia and the fear in her face made him want to die. Without a word he quickly turned and went back to his room and slammed the door.

In the morning he came out and found the kitchen cleaned and his aunt gone. He went out wearing the broken shoes in search of a way to fix things. There was no other way. On the streets what was once an asset became a liability as the shoes, broken from the train, shown like sores on his feet.

He searched as he never had in his life for a job, entering shop after shop, store after store, business after business, and each and every one showed him the door. On the streets what were stares of admiration and jealousy for Julio's footwear turned to scoffs and snickers as he shuffled his way in and out of doorways.

It could have all been in his mind, the shoes weren't so tragic, especially since Julio had spent an hour cleaning them and replacing the laces on the one. But to Julio, the world had turned against him. His hopes for a job were slim. No education. No experience. He walked in expecting to be rejected and in service of his wishes he was; again and again. A dark cloud formed around Julio. His eyes dimmed beneath a shroud of doubt and hatred for all things.

He entered a shop heavy with anger and suspicion. It was a smaller boutique selling house-wares on the Upper East Side. Julio went in and ran his fingers across the face of a shinny frying pan. He picked up a salt shaker and set it down. Everything was so shiny and new and the prices were beyond anything he imagined possible for such things. When he turned he found himself face to face with a clean-cut sales associate.

"Um," said the sales associate, "can I help you with something?"

Julio felt the blood rise, flushing his face. He tried to hide it, but he couldn't. He thought of his aunt and his cousins and for them he replied, "Yes, I'm looking for a job."

The sales associate smiled.

"Well..." he said, "we're not exactly hiring right now."

"What are you doing then," said Julio, "exactly?" showing the associate the sign he'd picked off the window that read, 'Seeking Sales Associate'.

The associate took a step back.

"Well, I don't know," he stammered, "you can wait for the manager if you want. But, you have to wait outside."

It wasn't the first time he'd been asked to wait outside for the manager. He hated all of this; the begging for a meaningless job with meager pay and no respect. Then to have to wait outside for an hour for a person to come who would take one look at him, toss an application his way and never call back. The rejection was constant, impersonal and cut him down every single time, deflating his ego bit by bit until only the empty weight of it remained to be dragged lifeless through the streets like a great heavy burden upon his soul.

Julio said nothing and just stared at the associate. He wanted the man to say something. Tell him something different. Provoke him so he could beat him down. Anything, just give me some kind of response. Something!

"Um," said the associate finally, uncomfortable himself. "Outside is that way," he pointed toward the door.

Julio turned and walked out the store and passed another shop with a help wanted sign prominently displayed in the window. He passed it with his eyes straight ahead. He passed with the purpose of someone who would not be denied. He passed one and then another and then went down into the train and headed back to 116th.

Rafa played as the sun warmed his face and hands. It felt good to be outside in the sun with the skin of the drums taught beneath his fingers. They always behaved different with the sun shining upon them. He played with a smile on his face, the rhythms rolling in a studiously efficient stream, clean against the haze of the afternoon sky and the bustle of 116th in the hot afternoon.

He kept time with almost surgical precision, enjoying the clean inspired response of the drums. Acting in kind with their mood, he closed his eyes and felt the air around him as the sounds eased out into the ether, the rhythms themselves flowing like slow smoke to fill the cracks and crevices of the surrounding streets as they explored with the edges of their precise sound.

By feeling the rhythms Rafa perceived the afternoon energies, both lazy and active, in search of itself, at peace with the day and the way it quietly passed minute by minute into oblivion. He played and with eyes closed became the streets around him, so that eventually his consciousness became the sounds of the drum bouncing off the walls of the buildings and filling the air. So much so that he lost the sense he was even playing at all; his hands becoming distant clouds from which the thunder of rhythms came, as if created by the creator himself. In this space he floated and in this way he played, embodied by the movements of the streets.

Suddenly, he became aware of a change in the rhythm. It came as if a third hand had entered his playing space. It was a dissonant counter rhythm that slapped the skins in violent protest. It became stronger and because it demanded Rafa's attention he came back to his hands and the features of his body and taking control reduced the rhythms to a whisper.

As his hands cooled, tapping lightly on the skins he opened his eyes and saw Julio come up out of the train station with his shoes that were once new but now destroyed and his eyes still dimmed by the dark cloud. Rafa stopped playing and leaned forward on his drums.

"Hey," he said when Julio came close enough, "you know what I think?"

Julio stopped for a second, "What?"

"You need some ice cream," he said, "to chill out."

"I got no time for your crap, old man," said Julio, walking on.

"I see you later, kid," said Rafa, but Julio was already down the block scanning the streets for Santos.

CHAPTER 6

Truth was, Santos wasn't a hard man to find. Not if you knew where to look, and Julio knew exactly where to look. But, he was a hard man to see.

Julio found Santos on his first try. He found him in the back of the barbershop on 125th. There were two men in the front of the shop that Julio recognized as Santos's right and left hands. They were ruthless cold-blooded killers, just like Santos.

One had a scar that ran from his forehead over his left eye to his lips. His name was Oscar. The scar brought up the corner of his mouth making it seem as if the man were constantly sneering, and the eye bent down in a scowl. Oscar never spoke. Some said they cut his tongue out in prison.

The other wore all black leather all the time. Not once had Julio seen him without the leather, not in winter or summer. He called himself Tony, even though Julio knew his name was Pedro. Tony was a good looking guy with slick hair and quick eyes. Both these guys carried guns and both of them would give their lives to protect Santos.

Julio came into the shop, the bell ringing behind him as he passed through the door. Oscar had been watching Julio come on from far away.

Tony was telling a story like he always was; he could talk for five men. He turned, and recognized Julio from the block.

"Hey kid, what you doing here?" he said.

Julio could see Santos in the back getting his hair cut. Santos had the shop to himself.

"Santos said to come see him," said Julio.

"That right?" said Tony. He smiled. "Them's some nice shoes you got, kid," he said and he smiled wise-guy style, "where'd you get em? You roll a bum, or something?"

Julio ignored him.

"More like he rolled you—I mean, look at your ragged ass." Tony thought that was pretty funny, but Julio wasn't laughing. He tracked Julio's eyes back to Santos, and then to Julio he said, "You too serious, primo, people like you don't live too long."

Julio looked at Tony and his smile and his leather suit, he'd always liked Tony's style, but right now he didn't care for him one bit.

"Can I see him or not?" asked Julio, his voice rising.

Tony took a couple steps towards Julio as his hand went up into his jacket.

"Chill," said Santos from the back. "Send the kid back, I want to talk to him."

Tony checked himself and with a dismissive wave sent Julio back. Julio's legs felt like Jell-O. When he got to the back of the shop he stopped short so Santos couldn't hear his heart pounding through his chest. Julio didn't want Santos to think he was too soft to work for him.

"Talk kid," said Santos as the barber worked his way around the chair.

"You know, like you said on the street, I wanna work," said Julio, trying his best to keep his cool.

"You need a job, eh?" He watched Julio in the mirror for a second. "I don't have no jobs for you," he said, finally.

Julio was crushed. His head went down and he felt his heart sink like a stone. He tried to raise his head, but his heart kept dragging it down. With nothing more to say, Julio began to walk off.

"Hold up, kid. Oscar might be able to help you find some work."

"Yea?" asked Julio, hopeful.

"Go with Oscar," said Santos.

Then, without even looking, Santos addressed his right hand man. "Oscar, take the kid job hunting. See he finds something nice."

Julio couldn't hold back the smile, "Yo, Santos, thanks bro."

"Nada, kid. Be cool."

Julio followed Oscar out of the shop and down the block they went. Julio felt proud to be walking the streets with Oscar. Everybody knew Oscar; he was almost as famous as Santos himself. As they walked, people got out of the way and Julio felt for the first time the power that guys like Oscar, Tony and Santos lived with every day.

Oscar walked with a steady calm, never showing hurry or stress and the people either stepped out of his way or greeted him with massive respect. Julio couldn't help feeling as if it were the same for him, as if it were Julio and Oscar demanding all that respect, not just Oscar. And, he loved it. He loved the feeling of power and the feeling of respect. This was even better than the shoes. He was getting respect even though the shoes were a wreck. He'd fix that though, real quick. Maybe by the end of the week he'd have the new shoes and he'd be on his way.

They walked a few blocks towards the East River and entered a semi-run-down apartment house in the middle of a run-down block. Oscar pointed for Julio to lead the way up. The doorway downstairs was open and the place looked vacant, but Julio had the sense that there were many eyes watching him now. They walked up the steps past the first and second floors until they reached the top flight.

It was very dark and Julio felt afraid. He could barely see Oscar coming up the stairs behind him, but he could see well enough to spot Oscar with his hand inside his jacket and Julio knew well enough to know that Oscar probably had his hand on a gun. At the top of the steps Julio waited, his eyes slowly adjusting to the darkness of the hallway. When Julio turned he found Oscar, his gun pulled, motioning Julio back, down the hallway.

With his eyes on Oscar, Julio walked backwards with slow easy strides, down the hallway. He glanced back, but only so he wouldn't trip and fall. Other than the few glances, he kept his eyes on the gun pointed directly at his stomach. At the end of the hallway, Oscar stopped, and using the gun, motioned for Julio to open the door between them.

Julio's heart was going a hundred miles an hour. He put his hand on the doorknob and turned. Inside, it looked like an apartment somebody's grandmother would live in. It was filled with old furniture and paintings, none of which were of particular value. The scent of cooking carried in from the kitchen and filled the apartment with a sense of home. At that moment it seemed strange to Julio to feel hunger for the food, but he did. Julio could hear someone moving about in the kitchen. Oscar slipped in behind Julio, and only when a very skinny man Julio had never seen before came from opposite the kitchen into the living room, did Oscar put the gun away.

"What up, hermano," said the skinny man to Oscar.

They shook hands in the way that good friends do. The skinny man looked at Julio.

"Hey," he said.

"What's up," said Julio.

"Let's go in the back," said the skinny man, and both Julio and Oscar followed him back.

They all went into the back bedroom where the window was covered with heavy curtains. Julio noticed the curtain was open just a bit on the side. He walked over and pulled it away enough to see that from the window one could see everything happening on the street. It would have been nothing for the skinny man to see him and Oscar coming from way down the block. He was looking down on the street when a rough hand shoved him hard into the wall; he hit it and came off, falling to the floor.

"What the hell was that for?!" Julio yelled from the floor.

Oscar stood over him, shaking his finger.

"If there's one thing I've learned in this business, kid," said the skinny man, "it's don't touch."

Julio picked himself up off the floor and joined the skinny man and Oscar by the bed. The skinny man sat down on the bed.

"So what's it gonna be," he asked. Oscar indicated Julio with his head. "O.K." said the skinny man, "so you done this before, kid?" he asked.

"Yea, a couple times."

"Ya, sure," mocked the skinny man, "but have you done this with these guys?" he asked.

"Once," said Julio, and Oscar turned with a disbelieving glance. "With Tiny, remember? I worked with Tiny."

Oscar shrugged, but the skinny man seemed satisfied.

"O.K., so you worked with Tiny," said the skinny man, "A hundred?" he asked, probing Oscar. Oscar didn't move. "Two hundred?" and Oscar was as still as a statue. The skinny man watched Oscar and shook his head, "Five hundred?" he asked and Oscar nodded.

"Well," said the skinny man again. "You must be some kind of kid, cuz that's a lot of product."

He went under the bed and from a duffle bag pulled out five zip-lock bags full of individually wrapped crack rocks.

This wasn't the first time Julio had seen crack, but it was the first time he would be touching it and selling it. The job he did for Tiny was all weed. He'd never sold crack before. Not any real crack, at least. The skinny man tossed the bags to Julio and he dropped two of them. He picked them up.

"This is the way it works," he said to Julio, "you go down there on the street where I can watch you, and you sell. Five bucks a baggie. When you're done you'll have five hundred dollars in your pocket. When you have that, come back and give me the money. You get two hundred—not too bad for a couple hours work."

"I got it," said Julio, stuffing the bags into his pockets.

Oscar pointed his thumb towards the door.

"You know what that means, kid," said the skinny man, "time for work."

Julio went out passed the grandma living room and out the door into the darkened hallway. He didn't like having all that crack in his pocket. He knew if he were to get busted by the cops right then he would be doing some serious time. Either that or he'd have to roll over on Santos and Oscar and the skinny man. But, he knew that was a sure death sentence. He didn't want to think about it so he thought about the money that would get him a new pair of sneakers.

First he would pay his aunt though. That was first. Help with the rent. Then he could get the shoes. But if he could sell all the crack real quick then he might just get the shoes first then sell some more for his aunt. He would wait and see.

He came out of the building into the late afternoon and set up on the corner. He'd heard how some dealers hid their stash so nobody would rob them, but Julio felt confident that this was Santo's turf and that nobody would mess with him there. Plus, it was crack and he had no idea how to sell crack. He ducked behind the fence of the broken lot and opened up a Ziploc baggie. There were a bunch of the little bags inside. He emptied them all into his pocket and tossed the Ziploc to the ground. Then he went out again to the corner to sell.

A crack addict came up with a bunch of change, but was about seventy cents short. Julio sent him on his way. Another came up about five minutes later with ten dollars and Julio walked him back behind the fence and took his money and gave him the rocks. Then the word got out because the crack-heads started coming in droves. Pretty soon, he didn't even have time to return to the corner and the crack heads just kept coming. He'd never seen so many. In about a half hour he was nearly out of drugs and his back pockets were bulging with cash. Julio checked the little bags in his pocket and counted out five more. Five more and I can go get my money, he said to himself, smiling.

He looked up and noticed there was nobody else coming. For a moment he got scared that the rush was over and that he would have to spend more time on the corner. But then, three men came around the fence and walked up to him.

Before Julio could move, two of them pulled out guns while the third went through Julio's pockets.

"Yo man, just don't shoot," said Julio.

"Shut up!" said the guy in his pockets.

Julio held his hands high, hoping they wouldn't shoot. Their eyes looked empty and crazed from fiending for the drugs. Julio had the sense that they were unaware themselves of what was happening. He thought about making a break for it or grabbing at one of the guns. As if sensing his thoughts, the guy on his left jumped forward and pulled Julio to the ground by the hair.

He pushed the gun into Julio's eye socket and held it there.

"You even think about it, kid, and you brains gonna leave a big alley cat mess right here."

The third man finished cleaning Julio's pockets and then, putting the guns away, the three walked smooth past the gate and disappeared.

Julio had nothing now. He picked himself up off the ground and dusted his clothes off. Out on the street things were as before.

"Yo, kid," said a man, Julio jumped back, his fists instinctively coming up to guard.

"What do you want?" Julio's voice nearly broke.

"What you think, son," said the man, smiling, "I want the good stuff."

"I'm out."

"Come back later?" asked the man.

"Sure, whatever," said Julio, as he pushed by the man.

He walked back to the house of the skinny man and the darkened hallways. This time when he went up the stairs there was even less light in the hallway, and even after he paused for a few seconds to let his eyes adjust, he still felt the place to be seriously dark and frightening. How could this guy live here, he asked himself, and with his woman, or his grandmother or whatever she was. How could he stay in a place like this with her?

He climbed to the third floor and felt his way down the hallway. He knocked on the door and waited. A woman answered, she was older, but not much older than Julio and she was so skinny, she couldn't have weighed more than 80 pounds.

"Oh, you the kid, right?" Her voice was like a spray of gravel.

"Yea."

She held the door, but Julio didn't move.

"Well, go on, he's in there."

She pointed to the same back bedroom as before.

Julio went through the living room and to the back bedroom. He knocked again and heard the skinny man say come in. So he did. The skinny man was coming away from the window and it occurred to Julio that he probably spent his entire life at that window, waiting and watching.

"That was pretty quick," said the skinny man, "you sold all of it, right?"

"Sold it all?" Julio was confused. He walked towards the window. "You didn't see that?" he asked.

"See what?"

Julio yanked back the curtain, "What do you mean? Didn't you see those guys rob me down there?!" he looked out the window and saw that from his perch up in the third floor window the skinny man could see every part of the street and neighborhood stretching out beyond, but he couldn't see back behind the fence where Julio was robbed.

"Right there!" Julio pointed, "Three guys came up and robbed me!"

The skinny man knocked the curtain out of Julio's hand.

"Yo, shut that!" he said. "And stop talking bull. What are you trying to say?" he added, rubbing his jaw furiously with his hand, "Nobody robbed you! I watched you from right here. I stood right here," and he pointed to the ground by the window, "the whole time I seen you and nobody robbed you."

"I swear, them three guys, they had guns. One of them put the gun to my eye and said he would kill me if I didn't give him everything." Julio was talking the talk of a desperate man.

"Bull!" shouted the skinny man walking up to Julio, his face stopping only inches from Julio's, "You know what I think? You got robbed, sure, robbed by your own crew! When you go down there, you all gonna meet up and split it four ways."

"That's a damn lie!" said Julio, stepping up.

The skinny man pushed him, "Tell me I'm a liar again! I kill you, kid! Right here, I'll kill you. You aint nothing to me."

"Don't push me!"

The skinny man scoffed.

"You know what…"

He went for the bed with his hand dipping under the pillow and Julio with his speed and luck alone caught the skinny man's wrist just as his hand came up holding a huge pistol.

With his other hand Julio grabbed the gun and yanked it free and the skinny man hit him with a punch in the face and Julio went down to the side but came up with an elbow that caught the lurching skinny man clean under the chin and sent him flying back against a desk that crushed to tinder beneath him. The skinny man was dazed and groping for a handhold in the pile of desk debris.

Julio pointed the gun at him.

"I didn't steal nothing! I was robbed! There were three of them, they had a gun and they robbed me! You hear?!"

He held the gun nervously before him, pointing it at the skinny man who could not get up, could not find his feet, could not yet speak. Julio moved on his feet from side to side, his jaw working in clenches, his knees going liquid beneath him.

"I'm telling you the truth, man," Julio went on, "I didn't want to hit you, but you *got* to understand."

The door behind Julio creaked just enough so that he heard it. He spun just as the skinny girl came through with shotgun barrels first. She read everything in an instant, seeing her man down with Julio holding the gun she raised the barrel of the shotgun to fire and Julio leapt to the side just as the barrel of the shotgun exploded with fire and deafening violence. Julio heard himself scream and for a moment he was sure he was dead, the gun had gone off so close to him that his eyes were streaked with the fire burst and his ears rang as if church bells hung from his head. He felt his heart pounding, then his arms and his legs and his hands and knew he had not been hit and with life threatening urgency he grabbed at the barrel of the shotgun just as the skinny woman raised it to fire again and yanked it free of her hands.

As he pulled, the gun went off and Julio felt it kick wild like a mule's leg kicking itself free of his hand and heard the pellets ricocheting like angry hornets off the floor and brick walls and felt them bouncing off his back. He acted instinctively, throwing the gun down and firing one-two-three solid punches into the skinny girl's face until she too went down in the doorway with her skirt up and her legs splayed impossibly skinny, impossibly tangled beneath her. He turned and saw that a shot, perhaps the first or the second, he didn't know which, had turned the skinny man's forearm to hamburger.

"Oh, man!" shouted Julio, "Oh, no!"

The skinny man was still trying to get up with his bloody arm like a brush full of red paint dabbing and smearing the floor beneath him. Julio turned and ran out and through the house. He stopped at the front door; everything inside of him was screaming *RUN! RUN! RUN!* But he turned and ran back into the bathroom and tore a towel off the rack and ran into the bedroom. The skinny man was still moving, but less than before.

"Here." said Julio, wrapping the arm tightly with the towel, "Keep this on here, real tight," he grabbed the man's good hand and put it on the towel and squeezed.

Julio jumped up and grabbed the woman off the floor.

"Hey!" he yelled, "wake up!" she didn't move.

He lifted her in his arms and taking her into the bathroom set her in the shower. He turned on the water as strong as it would go. It came down in a rush, soaking her clothes and face and legs and in a moment she moved and turning to her side came awake. Julio turned off the water and pulled her over to him. Her eyes came around and recognized him.

She started to struggle, "NOOOO!" she began to scream.

"Relax!" shouted Julio and she listened. "He's hurt. You shot him. You got to help him."

She got up and stumbling to the door looked over at the skinny man.

"Noel!?" she wailed, "Oh, my baby!"

"Listen!" said Julio, grabbing her and not letting her go, "I got robbed by three guys, I swear. You got to tell him that for me."

But she couldn't hear him anymore. She shook her head and tore herself free then went running across the room to Noel. Julio took a second to see her fall upon him and take his face into her wet hands.

Then Julio ran.

He ran as fast as he could out the door and down the steps and into the evening light that wasn't so dark he couldn't see the blood fresh and bright flashing left and right on his hands as he ran and ran, as fast as he could down the block, far as he could before he ran out of breath and stumbled into an alleyway back behind a dumpster where he collapsed heaving and shaking down amongst the refuse. He lay there for a moment catching his breath. He put his hand to his face and felt the blood smear in the sweat that poured from his skin. He jerked his hand back in alarm.

He'd forgotten the blood. He needed to get the blood off his hands. He needed to be free of it immediately. He leapt at a bag of garbage ripping it open and digging in the spilled entrails found a t-shirt which he used to frantically wipe the blood from his face and hands. He wiped so hard his skin burned with the scrapping of the fabric. He found a cup with some coffee in it and dumped the liquid into his hands and wiped it off with the shirt. All the while his mind spun away in a fury of thought. The cops were probably there now, he thought, at the house and if that guy dies there's no way she's going to say she shot him, so she'll say I shot him and then the cops will be looking for me and Oscar knows who I am and he'll know I didn't bring the money or the drugs and he'll think I killed that guy and then Santos will be looking for me.

The weight of it all was choking him. He could barely breathe. Even if he didn't die he still thinks I robbed him, he went on, and he'll tell Oscar and Santos that I robbed him and then I came up and tried to kill him. He'll lie, I just know he'll lie, thought Julio, and then he wished that he had killed the skinny man. That dumb girl too! Then he could just disappear and run away to someplace far away from all this trouble.

He wanted to run away now but he had no money and no hope of escape. No matter what he would be caught, either by the police or by Santos. Julio rose to his feet and threw the t-shirt back in the garbage. He walked as if nothing had happened. His body felt numb as he walked, as if it were nothing but flesh, while in his mind the torrent of concerns ragged in a near deafening Hell-fire that at once became a burning wall of background. He felt like the walking dead.

He walked on through the neighborhood not caring about anything. He was beat. He'd been dealt a cruel and crushing death blow. Either the police would come to take him away or Santos would kill him. It didn't matter now; he was a dead man any way he looked at it. Tightness in his stomach and a coursing sickness in his veins came to his attention. He spun to the side and threw up. He tried to care about what was going to happen, but he couldn't find a place to.

As he rounded the corner he heard something that caught his ear. It was distant, soft in the air at first, a sound completely foreign and separate from the sounds going on inside him and from the sounds of the neighborhood he knew. He walked on and the sound became louder. He recognized the sound of the drums now, but the rhythm was altogether new. It seemed to enter into his body and pull him along.

He felt it untying the knots in his stomach and the feeling come into his feet and hands and then to his legs as he moved closer and closer to the sound. Now he could hear the slaps of the rhythm and the subtler mid tones as they weaved in and out of the deep bass that beat steady as a heart behind it all. Slowly, his torso and his shoulders come back and finally as he walked into the public garden and closer to the sounds he felt his heart come again into his body and with it the grief for the skinny man and the girl and he felt his own grief for failing to abide by his aunt who wanted what was best for him and what he himself knew to be true.

The garden was a small one, going back into the block between two run down brownstone buildings. At the front there was a maze of vegetables and flowers and a tree that grew up strong with the green leaves dangling in the breeze. He went past all that to the casita at the back. It was a typical casita, built from scrap lumber with a small porch under roof for sitting in the rains. It had a hammock hung from the posts of the porch and Julio walked slowly now past the casita to the very back where he found himself face to face with Rafa, the old man from the subway stop seated at his drums.

He played a second more with his eyes closed and his face loose and relaxed then he abruptly stopped and opened his eyes.

"Hello, kid," said Rafa, not seeming surprised at all to see him standing there.

Julio didn't know what to say. Part of him wanted to run again, he wanted to run so bad, but part of him was curious and wanted to stay to ask Rafa what he was playing, so both parts were paralyzed and he could only stand there and stare.

"You like what I was playing?" asked Rafa, after a moment.

"What was that?"

"No name, no name for that music."

"Where does it come from?"

"I pulled it out of the air," said Rafa, and he made as if plucking something from thin air.

"Can you do it again?" asked Julio.

"Like that? Exactly?" he said and he smiled, "I could try, but what's the point?"

Julio sat down on the porch and looked around the garden. It was a nice place to be. There was a bird singing in the tree at the front and the place was cooler than on the street with a soft breeze that blew and Julio sat there with the old man in the fading light of the day, a day that had been a long and hard one for Julio and he was happy to be in such a nice place where he felt safe and calm. It had been a long time since he felt so safe and calm.

"Who owns this place?" asked Julio.

"Nobody," said the old man, "it was a dump, I cleaned it with some friends and now it is a garden. A place to sit and listen."

"Why?"

"Because it is necessary." The old man moved over to the porch with Julio, he pointed here and there with a wide opening of his hands, "This was life in Puerto Rico many years ago. You came to places like this to pass the day and eat food from the garden. Everybody had some place like this, some little land where the garden grows. You sit, play the drums, sing some songs. A place like this makes us people, you know."

But Julio didn't know. Life for him was the kitchen in his aunt's apartment and the battles for pride and reputation on the streets. He'd heard the stories from his aunt and some of his uncles about life in Puerto Rico, how things had changed so much, but he didn't have time for it. None of it seemed real to him, it was just a bunch of old people bitching about how things were.

"You know," said Rafa after some time had passed, "I played that rhythm special for you."

Julio sucked his teeth in disbelief.

"Sure, I did. I used it to call you here."

"Ya, right," said Julio. The old man was nuts.

"You can deny all you want, but a truth is a truth," said Rafa.

Julio felt strange that the old man would say such a thing, much stranger that he would actually do such a thing—that is if he really could.

"You sick, Julio. I can see it in you. You are sick with the money sickness."

Julio didn't remember telling the old man his name, "The money sickness?" he asked, "What you talking about?" and he came off the porch to face Rafa in the garden.

"You sick, you know like a sick man, you have money and all this stuff on your mind all the time, I see you walking like a blind man in the streets."

"Like a blind man?!" Julio said, "Man, I don't have time for this crap," and he made as if to leave.

"Where you going, kid?" said Rafa, "Aint nothing out there for you anymore."

Julio stopped and turned, "Why you all up in my business, old man?"

"Why don't you cool that attitude of yours, eh?!" Rafa stood and faced Julio, "You make me so tired with that crap," Rafa pointed at him, "and, you tired too, you tired of that crap too."

Julio took a deep breath. He was tired of it. He could feel it now that the old man said it. He was tired of running and fighting for everything in his life and still his life felt empty. He went over and sat back on the porch of the casita and looked down at the shoes that had meant so much to him. When he looked at them he felt the need to get another pair.

These were so ugly and had so much damage to them. But they were comfortable and looked like they still would last a long time.

Wasn't that enough? No, he heard himself say, they had to look good too, so that people would know he was someone to be respected. He had to have his respect, on the streets you die without respect. On the streets there is nothing else. If someone disrespects you then they must go down hard and fast.

Julio looked up at the old man. It was getting dark and he could barely see his face in the diffused light of the far off street lamps. He looked haunted in the light with his beard and wild hair.

"What else is there, man? There's money, and power, and respect and what else is there?" Julio wanted to know.

"The language of the drum, mijo," said Rafa.

"The drum has a language?"

"Sure, it talks to you, tells you things you need to know. Shows you things. It's like your guide. If you don't learn the language, you can't be happy, because then you lost."

"You know the language?" asked Julio.

"Know it?" scoffed the old man, "I speak with the drums every day."

"Can you do it now?"

"You know it," said Rafa.

"Play it now."

Rafa smiled.

"How bout I play a song to get rid of your money sickness?" suggested Rafa, as he made his way in the faded light towards the drums.

"I don't want to hear no Santería Voodoo bull."

"Who said anything about Voodoo?" said Rafa, "I said a song."

He sat at the drums and very lightly began to play. The light tapping sounded like rain hitting the roof at the beginning of a storm. But there was a skip to it, moving the raindrops across the roof with subtle clicks of pitch that ran around Julio making him smile. Then the bass came in, totally unexpected in full compliment of the taps and again it rang and pretty quick the whole rhythm was taking shape around the rain sound and Julio found his foot tapping to the beat and then Rafa began to sing.

He didn't sing any words. They were more like long wailing chants that built beautiful bridges between the beats of the drum.

His voice was rough and old sounding like the warn edges of a wooden table, but it had a smoothness to it too, almost as if the roughness to it were contained in the color, not the texture. Julio liked the old man's singing with the sound of the drums. It was not a happy song, but it wasn't sad either. He felt himself in the middle of both, content to sit there next to the old man with his drums. Rafa played for a few seconds more and then with a very short and understated flurry, stopped.

"Ya," said Rafa, letting out a deep breath before sitting back, relaxed behind the drums.

Julio didn't know what to say. He felt like hugging the old man. Then just as quick he knew what his boys would say if they found him hanging out in the public garden with the crazy old man drummer, Rafa. They would never let him live it down. Then he remembered that Santos would probably kill him before he got home and he felt his insides crash down like a tower of broken bricks. Not knowing what to do or where to go, Julio got up slowly and shrugged.

"Nice try old man, but I got to go."

And he walked off.

"Hey kid," said Rafa, and Julio stopped and turned his head,

"Some things take time to work themselves out, mijo. Magic isn't magic, you know."

Julio laughed at that, "You crazy, man. You crazy," he said and passed between the gates of the garden to the street.

He wished he felt different about things but he was afraid he never would. Chances of surviving the revenge of the skinny man, Oscar, and most of all, Santos, were slim.

Conscious to the rhythm of his stride, Julio found himself replicating Rafa's song as he walked. His heart warmed as if in contact with a bright and warm light. He found his troubles fading from his mind. With Rafa's song strong in his heart there was no room for anything else, so Julio went along with it willingly. For some reason he was able to replicate the chorus quite accurately. Light as a feather on his lips he sang it with cautious awareness. It felt good.

"Magic isn't magic," he said to himself with a smile.

CHAPTER 7

In the light of his aunt's kitchen he saw instantly that he was a mess. There was still blood in dark lines outlining his fingernails. He stunk of coffee and garbage and sweat. Lucky for Julio, Sylvia was at the stove cooking and had her back to him when he came in. Quick as he could, he slipped by her and into the bathroom.

When he emerged at least his hands and face were clean. He wished he could put his whole life in that little bathroom sink and wash it clean of the troubles that soiled his heart and mind now.

Careful to follow all the protocol, Julio quietly pulled the chair out and sat straight with his hands in his lap and his back erect.

"Well, you arrived just in time," said Sylvia, not turning.

"Where are my cousins?" asked Julio.

"They all went down to the library to do their homework." She stirred the pot, "They'll be back later."

Julio sat still, shrinking and waiting.

Finally, Sylvia with a steaming pot of chicken stew turned and began filling the plate before Julio. When she looked up, she paused at his face.

"I don't know what you did, but you look guilty."

"What?" he said, and sat up straighter.

"That look on your face. Like you finally got caught," she said.

She sat and took a bite, letting the silence fill the room.

Julio looked at his plate and didn't feel like eating anymore. He forced himself to take the spoon into his hand and pushed it lifelessly into the stew that was steaming and filling the air with home cooked aromas. His aunt's food was better than good, better than most.

Out of the corner of her eye she watched him. Putting her own spoon down, she picked up her napkin and with dainty dabs cleaned the corners of her mouth.

"So what? What is it? No job, eh?"

"No" said Julio, his face lowering.

"Well," she said, "you better eat. Otherwise you'll be too tired to look tomorrow." Julio fell a few steps lower and she sensed it.

"Listen," she continued, "looking for work is hard—I know." When he looked up, she continued, "You'll find something, Julio. You just have to keep looking."

Then she went back to eating her stew.

Reluctantly Julio lifted the spoon filled with the chicken stew and tasted it. He ate mechanically with the eyes of his aunt upon him. He tried not to think of the skinny man with his bloody arm and the skinny girl with her nose bloodied and broken with her legs splayed out, and he tried not to think of Santos and Oscar who could be on their way up to the kitchen to kill him right now. He tried not to think of the violence and dangers of the day and so he pushed with all his might to get these things out of his head and all the while he fed his mouth with a tasteless, passionless labor.

From a distant corner of his heart he heard the drums again, as if Rafa were playing down the block. He heard the song come up again, filling him gradually, and with it the melody of Rafa's voice. In seconds the tension held in his legs began to subside. Chasing the beat he filled his body with the song until all the worries of the day ebbed away. He felt his foot tapping the floor and the taste of the food came into his mouth as he delved deeper and deeper into the rhythm of the song.

With his plate cleared, Julio picked up his dishes and washed them clean in the sink. While he was at it, he washed the remaining dishes in sight too. When he turned, his aunt was staring at him, a slight smile forming on her lips.

There was a knock at the door and Julio's heart leapt into his throat.

The knock came again—impatient, pounding.

Julio inched along the counter towards the hallway, his mind filling with the fear of what was to come until it bellowed and screamed like the passing of a runaway train. With all the sounds of Rafa's song gone, Julio was run flat with fear.

Sylvia stood, "Who the hell knocks like that?" she said.

She caught Julio's face out of the corner of her eye and turned full on him.

"What's wrong with you?" she demanded.

He didn't move.

"What are you so scared of?"

Before she could say another word the pounding on the door came up again.

"Ya!" she screamed at the door and Julio jumped with her shout.

Turning to the door she went and looked out the peep hole,

"There's nobody there," she said, "Who's there?" she said to the door, and then began to turn the locks on the door.

Julio wanted to stop her, to tell her to just let them stay outside, he wanted to warn her, but he couldn't move. The words 'don't do it' caught in his throat like meat hooks ripping his insides out and so he just watched with fear crushing the corners of his mouth and eyes.

She opened the door and Julio's cousin, the younger of the two girls, pushed her way in.

"Jeeze mom, leave me outside why don't you," she said as she tossed her books to the floor and sat at the table.

"Where's your sister and brother?" asked Sylvia.

"They're being stupid, so I left."

"You walked home alone?" she asked her daughter.

Her daughter gave her a look, "I can handle it, mom."

Sylvia picked up the book bag and set it on the chair, "Don't do that again," she said, and then she walked over to the stove to serve her daughter dinner.

Julio looked in on the kitchen and his aunt with her daughter and moved silently away down the hallway to his room. Once there, he shut the door and threw himself face down on the bed.

If Santos came to his aunt's place she would never, ever forgive him. He would never forgive himself. He might as well let Santos kill him right there because if he didn't, his aunt would certainly do it for him. He knew from stories that he could not bargain with Santos. He knew that once activated, Oscar could not be stopped. He knew from experience that Santos was not above taking out punishment on a family member to make a point to someone who was hiding. All these thoughts clouded his mind when a knock came to his door and his aunt let herself in.

"So," she began, "someone is looking for you?" her words were thick with sorrow and hate.

Julio turned over to face her. She stood erect in the doorway.

"Someone wants to hurt you?" she asked.

Julio brought his hands up behind his head on the bed and shrugged his shoulders.

She came in, quietly shutting the door behind her. Grabbing a chair from the desk, she pulled it up alongside the bed and sat down. She took a breath and gave Julio a long look.

"If you bring your evil into my house…"

Her tears cut her off.

Only by choking them in her throat and biting them back off her lip was she able to hold them in.

She waited a moment more, then, "My babies," she said, but the thought was too much for her and the tears came again.

Julio couldn't say anything.

He didn't want to see her cry. But he knew there was nothing he could say at that moment to make her feel better. He knew what he had to do and it had nothing to do with his aunt Sylvia. As the moment wore on he felt himself sink lower and lower into depression until somewhere down at the bottom the anger kicked in and he wanted his aunt out of his room right then.

A rage came rising where the guilt had been, a rage born of the constant disappointments, the constant failures, the constant bickering with his aunt. He was tired of feeling at the bottom and more than anything he wanted up and out of his misery. His anger rose as he lifted himself to face his aunt, he wanted to tell her to get the hell out of his room with all her crying. He wanted to tell her to leave him alone. He cleared his throat and she looked at him with her watery eyes and in that moment he lost all his will and the anger fell inside returning him to a place of deep depression, guilt and anguish.

She stared at him and in her eyes he could see the disappointment and the concern and in the mouth he could see the anger building and he knew that at any moment she might explode and begin slapping him. She was so close to him, sitting on his bed, so close he knew if she began to hit him it would be a real struggle to get her off, and he was afraid again that if the anger rose inside like it had just done, he would hit her like the skinny girl, and he knew he would not stop until it was too late.

So he did the only thing he could, he rolled over and curled up in a ball and waited.

After some time she went out, leaving him alone with his mind and the endless ringing of the nightmare images it provided him. He waited for sleep, but it never came.

CHAPTER 8

In the morning he went to the kitchen and found her there waiting. By the bags under her eyes he knew that she had not slept much either. Steam rose from her coffee cup and twisted serpent like from between her clasped hands.

"So." She began. "What are you going to do now?" The sadness from the night before was long gone. Only the anger was evident.

Julio knew he was on thin ice. He knew that she was like a cornered wild animal right now. He had to say the right thing or she would explode on him. She was waiting for that. She wanted to explode on him. She wanted to have a giant fight with him so that he would leave.

Then he heard Rafa's drums come from out of nowhere, filling the spaces within him. They were happy and full of hope. Slowly, the building pressures ebbed away as the song filled him with rhythmic bliss.

He tried to stop himself, but he couldn't.

"I was thinking, maybe I'll buy a drum and learn to play it," he announced.

Her mouth dropped open.

"What?" she said, "Are you crazy?"

"I want to learn the drum," he repeated, less sure.

"Perfect!" she said, slamming down her coffee. "Take the rent money, we don't need it!"

And just like that, the fuse had reached the charge.

"With all your problems and mine, you think of buying things!" She was standing now, pacing back and forth in front of him, "A drum!" she shouted, "You are never going to be a man, you know." She was in his face now, "You're a punk! A stupid street punk! You have no idea what it means to be a man!"

He could feel the rage coming up inside him. Never had it come so strong and so quick. Never had he wanted to hurt his aunt as he did now. He turned away from her to avoid what was coming, but that only made her angrier.

"You look at me when I'm talking to you!" she demanded. "You're worthless!" she screamed. But Julio kept his face away, his eyes away, and his mind like a cork on the rage that seemed to be bursting from within.

Then she slapped him—hard, on the side of the head. His ear exploded with pain and with the pain he could control it no longer. In one quick motion he leapt to his feet and shoved her with everything he had.

She went flying across the kitchen and slammed brutally hard into the low cabinets, breaking dishes and spilling items in a confetti like crash that showered her flailing body. She went down, falling finally to the floor where she knelt on hands and knees, heaving for breath and clarity. He leapt forward to kick her in the guts but somehow managed to stop himself just in time. Julio took a halted step back and saw his aunt broken on the floor and the kitchen again dismantled by their fights and the sight of it all was like a knife in his heart.

He ran to his room and quickly stuffed his school bag with some clothes and things and putting on the broken sneakers he walked out. At the kitchen he paused for a moment. His aunt was sitting on the floor, her eyes closed and her hand holding her injured back.

Compassion rushed in on every side stopping Julio further.

"Are you o.k. tía?" he asked.

She just sat there, her eyes closed, holding her side.

"Tía?" he probed.

"Get out!" she screamed, "Get out of my house. And, never come back!"

Rage welled up inside him again, and so looking away he headed for the door and without looking back went out, slamming it behind him.

On the street he remembered Santos and became suddenly aware of dangers far greater than his aunt. He moved quick, but not too quick, sliding in and out of doorways, his eyes alert and his heart beating fast. He didn't know where he was headed, but he knew he must get out of the neighborhood for good. If Santos found him it would mean a certain, instant, and most definitely painful death.

Quickly, he moved through the neighborhood, the neighborhood he had known throughout his youth. It was the only place he'd known in life. He felt his heart sadden as he moved through and away from his home.

Rafa's song came again into his mind. Building in layers, the music took over his thoughts leaving him fixed on the rhythms rather than on his troubles. With the stress ebbing away, Julio was faced with the fact that above all, he must decide on a destination, otherwise he might wonder aimlessly until he crossed Santos or fell flat on his face.

Julio thought of the possibilities for his constricted future but found only the hollow ring of a clear and empty sky. He heard the drums again, coming from somewhere in that emptiness he knew only as the future. The sounds of the drums and the melodies of Rafa's song reminded him so much of Puerto Rico—a place he knew only in drawings made by optimistic little child like fingers on the escaping dust of memory—that it became a place, real or otherwise, where he knew at once he must go.

Of course, he said to himself, Puerto Rico! It would be the place for him. No more Santos, no more tia, no more trouble. He could get a job and move in with his cousins. I know I have some cousins somewhere down there, he said to himself. I must have, he convinced himself. Tia would know. I'll just call her when I'm there and ask, he decided.

The images of white sand beaches and palms languidly waving him in on the trade winds, with sea clear blue and inviting, bikini girls coming and going with permanent grins; it all filled his mind, and there, on the sands of his imagination, he saw himself dressed in white, drinking a tropical drink, listening to the drums of his people in his homeland with a girl tethered to each side by slender bronze arms basking in the sun. He felt the music building in layers across his mind as the sun of his imaginary Puerto Rico warmed his heart and soul.

He suddenly got the idea to seek out Rafa, and so he went with guarded care to find him in the garden. Rafa would know about Puerto Rico. He would know how to get there. But most of all, Julio somehow knew Rafa would understand the need to follow his dreams, no matter how fanciful.

CHAPTER 9

When he came upon the garden, he looked in and saw Rafa in the back, preparing what looked like breakfast. Julio went in, his bag bulging on his back.

Rafa looked up from his frying pan.

"Hey, kid, you up early."

Julio wearily put his bag down on the steps to the casita.

"What you got in there?" Rafa asked, before moving his attention back to his cooking.

"Everything."

"Everything?" Rafa contemplated that, then nodded.

"I'm running away," said Julio.

Rafa didn't even look up, "Really?" he said.

Julio looked around nervously.

"Yea, things are bad with my aunt, she's not letting me be the kind of man I want to be, so I decided I got to go."

"That right?" said Rafa, moving about the stove.

Julio felt awkward, his plan to come see Rafa making less sense by the moment. Finally Rafa stopped and looked up at Julio and smiled.

"So, if you running away, what you doing here?" he asked.

Julio didn't really know, but a thought occurred to him, so he said, "I though you could teach me some beats, you know, so when I get to Puerto Rico I can play the drums and stuff."

Rafa smiled, watching Julio shift his weight from one foot to the other.

"You know, a little something quick, something I could build on."

"Sure kid, I can teach you some things," said Rafa, then he went back to cooking.

Julio sat down on the porch, and it wasn't such a bad place to be, so he waited for Rafa to finish cooking his meal. He knew it would be a long journey to Puerto Rico, maybe days. He didn't know. The train would be the best way to go, he thought, but he didn't know where to catch the train. He knew he would have to get across the water from Florida, but there had to be a boat or something, he thought. Maybe a bus would be better after all, probably cheaper than the train. He'd have to save money to make it. Of course he'd have to make some money first before he could save it. There had to be some way to make some quick money, he thought. He wondered how much it would cost and he wondered how long it would take to get there. Julio was about to ask Rafa what would be the best way to get to Puerto Rico when he spoke up.

"O.K." said Rafa, forking the bananas from the frying pan to a pile on the plate by his side. "Almost there."

From an adjacent pan Rafa spooned delicate white rice onto a plate. From another he pulled two boiled eggs and pealing them quickly with practiced hands placed them onto the rice. Then the bananas, fried golden brown with their sweet smell filling the morning, which he lifted by the ends with the fork, were placed along side the rice and eggs. Everything looked light and fresh and in no time Julio found his mouth was watering.

"Fried eggs, no good," said Rafa, as if he were talking to himself, or a studio audience, "boiled is better for the heart."

Without asking Rafa passed the plate to Julio with the fork still standing skewered in the end of a banana.

"Yo. I don't want to eat your food, old man," said Julio, holding the plate.

"You look like you do. You think I no cook good or something?"

"No man, not that. Just, what are you going to eat?"

Rafa smiled, "I made enough for two," he said. Lifting another plate and equaling the portions he served to Julio he added,

"You never know who might drop by."

Julio watched Rafa serve himself, and only when he was done serving and seated by his side did Julio begin to eat himself.

When Julio finished he felt good. With a full belly he sat back against the post on the porch and took in the garden morning.

"So," said Rafa, cleaning his mouth with a napkin from his pocket, "Puerto Rico, eh?"

Julio sat up, "Yea, I got some cousins down there, I think."

"Sure you do, kid."

"You know, I was born there."

"Me too." said Rafa. "Long trip."

"How long?"

"Oooooo, days, weeks. Depends."

"Man, that's long." Julio shook his head.

"But worth it," assured Rafa.

"Yea?"

"It's the mother land, hijo. There is nothing like it. You don't remember?"

"Nah. Too young."

"I was young too, but I'll never forget her. The simple life, you know—music, good food, good friends, good women." A knowing smile spread across his face as his voice tailed off to the pleasantries.

"That's what I'm talking about, yo!" Julio stood, he was getting excited, "Something different than here, I need that change, man."

"Yea, that's good," said Rafa with an even grander smile. "Change is good, kid. Real good."

Julio sat down again. He was too pumped up to stand, or sit. He didn't know which was better. All he knew was that he was excited about his pending journey to Puerto Rico. The old man had really stoked his fire.

Rafa changed gears.

"So you want to play the drum, eh?" asked Rafa.

"Yea, yea," said Julio, "I want to learn that stuff. Play some beats, you know. Like you do—that real deep stuff."

"You want me to play something for you now?" asked Rafa.

"Hell ya!" said Julio.

Rafa went over to the drums and sat down behind them. He slapped his hands together, *SMACK!* His palms flat, and rubbing them briskly, he created a swishing sound not unlike a muted shaker. At first the rhythm of his hands was monotonous, metronome like, and very fast. But then a groove began to form in the palms of his hands and what had a moment before appeared to be some kind of warm-up became the introduction to a song. Rafa closed his eyes and allowed the sounds to fill his ears.

Julio watched him unable to take his eyes away.

Rafa let the sounds pour over him, enveloping him. He felt the waves come off his hands and like rings from a stone tossed into a quiet pond, the sound from his hands traveled outward into the world. He felt the boy seated at the porch with his attention on him. He felt the birds in the treetops above. He felt the casita in all its age and wisdom. And, as always, out beyond the fence he felt the street, with its dangers and violence and its communal warmth.

He moved his hands with the rhythms that came to him from the spirits of these things, allowing them to dictate the sounds. From a short distance he felt the urge come, clear as a bright sunny day, and when it came he hit the drums with a quick strike, then back with his hands, shaker-like with the rhythm.

From Julio's perspective the whole thing was like an orchestrated show, as if Rafa had written the song before and was now playing it for him. Except that he felt himself in the song, or rather he felt as if the song were a perfect fit for him. It paralleled his emotion, his fear of the streets and his apprehension for his future. When Rafa went to the skins of the drums, creating bold strikes that punctuated the rhythm with gunshot pops and thunderous rumblings, Julio was reminded of his troubles with Santos and his aunt and not even the lingering dream of a Puerto Rican escape diminished his growing anxiety. The rhythms were tribal, raw, and bold, and when Rafa began to sing in a minor key with his gravely voice almost a whisper, it brought a well of emotions up in Julio to the point that he felt at any moment he might break out crying.

Puerto Rico was a fantasy and he knew it. Even the cousins were a fantasy. Faced again with his predicament at home Julio hung his head low, and his mood fit right in with the beat of the drum. He closed his eyes allowing himself to list with the groove, with the heaviness of his life driving down upon him.

Except that somewhere in the rhythm there was hope, Julio could hear it there, too. There was a bit of liveliness to it that came with a quick clicking off the side of the drum and Julio looked up and realized that the clicking was coming from Rafa's knee as it tapped the side of the drum. He knew that there was nowhere to run. There was nowhere he could possibly run to. But he also knew that there was hope for him someplace. Most of all he knew that the drums were speaking to him in a way that nothing had ever before in his life. They were like the voice of God. He wanted to play them like Rafa so that he could hear that voice every day.

Rafa finished the song and took a deep breath, then opened his eyes again.

"Thank you."

"No, mijo, thank you," said Rafa, smiling.

"You think you could teach me some of that?"

Rafa considered Julio's request. He was about to answer him, when it appeared he changed his mind.

"Don't you think you should get going?" he said, "Takes a long time to learn, and Puerto Rico is far."

Rafa came out from behind the drums.

"You're going to have to start that journey soon, or you'll waste that breakfast sitting here talking to me," he said.

Julio scratched his head, "Yea, I guess you're right."

"I mean, you going, no?" asked Rafa.

Julio stood again, "Sure, of course I'm going."

He half heartily reached for his bag. He didn't know where he would go next, but he knew Puerto Rico was an impossible long way off.

"I guess I'll see you around, then," said Julio.

"See you when you come back to visit."

"Yea," said Julio, not so sure, "I'll bring you some coconuts or something."

Rafa laughed, he liked that one. The two shook hands.

Julio turned to walk out the garden and found his legs heavy like rooted tree trunks beneath him. He took a few steps towards the gate and as the street came into view and broadened in sound and sight, he felt the dangers that awaited him, the uncertainty of his decision, and the hopelessness of his future. He stopped and turned.

"Hey, it might be too late to leave now, you know. Better to get an early start. Don't you think?" he asked.

Rafa considered this.

"Perhaps," was all he said.

"Ya, I think I'll go tomorrow," said Julio, "You know, then I can learn a little something, too. Go down there with a little something to show."

"Yea?" asked Rafa.

"Yea," said Julio.

"Pues, if you think its best, sure, do like you like," said Rafa with a smile, moving to the porch where he sat down on an old chair.

Julio joined him. "So, teach me some of that nasty stuff, man."

"Not that easy, kid." He said, "You no ready."

"So how do I get ready?"

Rafa rubbed his chin, "Let's see," he said, his eyes probing the empty sky, "I think it better if you have your own drum." Rafa thought a moment. He was silent, within himself. Finally he spoke.

"Yea. First, you need your own drum."

Julio's face dropped.

"Man, how am I supposed to get a drum?" he pushed away, "You know I don't have any money, man. Look at my shoes."

"You're shoes look good," said Rafa, "good and broken." Rafa laughed at his own joke.

"Don't play with me, old man."

Rafa stopped laughing, "I didn't say go *buy* a drum, I said you *need* your own drum." Rafa was firm, but patient with Julio. "You need to learn the language of the drum, without that, you playing nothing, mijo. You playing nothing but yourself. The way to learn is using your own drum."

Julio sucked his teeth.

"Man, where am I going to get a drum?"

"You no fun, kid," said Rafa. He sat back a moment. A thought came to him.

"You know what," he said.

"What?"

"You need some wood."

"Wood? You're crazy. What, am I gonna build a boat and sail to Puerto Rico?!"

"No, mijo. Better," and Rafa's smile was grand indeed. "You going to *build* your own drum."

Julio fell back in laughter, "Man, you're crazy. No doubt! I mean—I can't build nothing."

But, he could see that Rafa wasn't kidding.

"Of course you can," said Rafa, simply.

Julio didn't buy it, not one stinking word of it.

"Build a drum, yea. Sure, old man. Whatever you say." he said, but Rafa was unmoved by Julio's skepticism.

Julio toyed with the zippers of his backpack, flicking them back and forth between his fingers as Rafa stood silent, watching.

Finally, Julio threw up his hands.

"Where am I going to get the wood? How am I going to build it?" he asked. "Man, why don't you just show me some beats and I'll get out of here."

"You want to play the drums like I do?"

"Yea."

"You want to learn how to make the drum talk?"

"Yea."

"So you can speak and understand the language of the drum?"

"Yea."

"Then go find some wood."

Julio grimaced, reluctant still.

"What else you got to do?" asked Rafa, and Julio knew there was nothing for him anywhere anymore.

The stupid fantasy drum and the old man were all he had.

Julio shook his head. A bird landed on a low branch before them and feeling the garden began to sing a melodic song. A breeze came down, warm, but comfortable, and on it the flowers spread their fragrant love song. Julio took all this in. The garden was a nice place to be, he decided.

"What kind of wood do I need?" asked Julio.

Rafa shrugged.

"How much do I need to get?" Julio asked.

"Hard to say," said Rafa.

"Well, how long will it take?" asked Julio.

"You never know," answered Rafa.

Julio scowled, "You a lot of help."

"Here, take my hat," offered Rafa, "It's hot out there, nice to cover your face." and Rafa passed him a broad brimmed straw hat with a single black band. It was in the old style, not uncommonly seen in the neighborhood. Julio thought not of the sun, but more of hiding from Santos.

"Yea, cool," said Julio, "good idea."

Julio set out to find the wood for the drum. He left his bag with Rafa back at the casita and hit the streets. Whether it was avoidance of Santos and his men or pure honest interest, all Julio could think of was learning the language of the drum so that he might play like Rafa one day.

In fact, he became so concentrated on searching for wood that he didn't even notice Santos seated at the back of a restaurant as he passed.

Lucky for Julio, at that very moment Santos was busy.

CHAPTER 10

Inside the restaurant, things were far less optimistic than within the mind of Julio. Tony, listening to Santos, held his head low and cleared the table a breadcrumb at a time with the tip of his finger.

"I want you two to figure out who's doing this!" demanded Santos. "Somebody's out there jacking my stuff every day. This keeps up, we all dead."

Santos looked up at Tony, then slapped him viciously across the face with his big, ex-football star hand. Tony nearly fell out of his chair, but he didn't say anything, he just came back up and played it cool.

"You slippin, kid. These guys are making a fool out of you, and that means they making a fool out of me. I go down, and you going too. You want that?"

"No."

"Well, things don't change, and real quick, then it gonna happen, killer. It going to happen to *you*."

Santos looked at Oscar as if to say the same went for him. But he didn't dare slap Oscar. He never put his hands on Oscar. Oscar always did what he was told and always delivered in stunningly efficient fashion.

"Big O here is gonna help you out, T. You need the help right now."

Tony looked up at Oscar, and again Oscar only nodded. This wasn't the first time Oscar had been called in to help, and it probably wouldn't be the last.

Santos seemed more relaxed after the slap and scolding.

"What about Noel?" asked Tony.

"He in the hospital?" asked Santos.

Oscar nodded his head.

"He gotta go," said Santos.

Tony leaned back, uneasy.

Santos picked up on his reluctance.

"You getting soft? Tell me you soft! Tell me you aint got the guts!"

Tony juggled the words in his mind a moment, trying to find a way to express himself without bringing down Santos's punishing wrath. The first part was the easy part.

"I aint soft. Not even close." Tony said, then he took a deep breath. "Listen, I never question your moves, bro. You the best. You know that. The best ever. Period. But he been your boy for a hot minute."

For Santos it was much simpler than all that.

"He talks, we go down." Santos stared into Tony's eyes, then Oscar's. "You hear?" he said, not wanting to hear another word.

Tony was going to say something, but Oscar stopped him with a hand under the table. When Santos looked up again Oscar gave him an easy reassuring nod.

"Why can't you be more like this guy?" said Santos, pointing a thumb at Oscar. "Another thing," he continued, "I want that kid. You can catch a kid, right?"

"He aint going nowhere," said Tony.

"Well, you find him yet?"

"No. But I know where he lives."

"Even I know where he lives, stupid." Santos looked over at Oscar again, "help him with this one too, will you."

Tony shook his head, "Yo. I can find a kid, alright."

"You don't piss unless I tell you to, you hear me! If I say Oscar's gonna help, then he gonna help!"

Tony sat back again, pouting this time.

Everyone at the table was silent. Everything that needed to be said had been said. Now they were alone in their heads, thinking about what would come. Tony knew it wasn't going to be pretty. He had a feeling, and a bad one. All this stunk, every last bit of it.

Santos thought about the kid, Julio, who he never saw coming. He never imagined that the kid could have robbed him so quick for so much. Not to mention Noel, who was one badass dude. How the kid had been able to go back up and work Noel for everything in the house was something he'd never understand. When all the dust settled, that little fiasco with Julio had cost Santos plenty. Santos never imagined Julio had that kind of skill or ambition. He didn't see it, and more than anything this bothered Santos, because he didn't miss much at all. You couldn't miss things like the volatile ambition of an underling and survive in this business, and Santos had more than survived. He'd excelled.

"That kid's working for somebody. Might even be his crew, who knows. All I know is, nobody robs from me and gets away with it. You hear me? Nobody."

CHAPTER 11

Rafa finished setting up his drums in his usual spot. He set out the bucket where people left the only money he ever made anymore. It wasn't much, but it paid for his food and an occasional item of clothing or element for his drum and that was plenty for him.

He felt good. It had been a good morning so far, as most were for Rafa. He smiled at the people who passed on their way to work and they smiled back. For many it would be the only smile of the day, a fact which Rafa realized, but one that made little impression on him.

Behind the drums Rafa warmed up to the day and what it would become. By rubbing his open palms across the skins he warmed his hands and his hands warmed the skins and the sound that came from the meeting warmed the hearts of those who passed by. Seated at the opening to the subway stop, he had a front row seat to the happenings of the neighborhood. It was a place he loved and his place there had become as natural to witness as the rising of the sun. Even in the rain, Rafa would set up under cover of the store awning where the shopkeeper, Felipe, happily sacrificed a corner of his outdoor display. If necessary, Felipe would bring out the umbrella he bought specifically to keep the rain off Rafa and his drums.

In this way, the whole neighborhood provided for Rafa. They needed his playing, as a day without the drums didn't seem like a day at all but more like a chore, or an endless string of meaningless interactions. As it seemed on those cold New York winter days, when not even the venerable Rafa could sit comfortably outside and play, but rather held out behind the piping hot stove of the casita, or hid himself in a kind neighbor's home. On those days, the streets void of Rafa's playing seemed extra cold and grey.

If Rafa were to ever disappear from his place at the subway opening, the neighborhood would eventually recover. It would live on, as all neighborhoods do. Rafa knew this as well as he knew the precious value of every moment of every day. It was this knowledge that brought him to the same place every day; the knowledge that at any moment everything in the world could be taken away.

But not today. Today was a sunny summer day. Today Rafa and his neighborhood were going to play.

CHAPTER 12

Julio walked uptown out and away from his barrio. He knew Santos was looking for him, but the danger seemed diminished in his hunt for the elements that would bring him a drum of his own. Right now that meant wood, and so Julio walked with his ears and eyes open for some sign that would bring him to his prize.

The day was warmed by a languid breeze that labored to move the strong smells of the city as they rolled in great overturned circles through the streets. Passing corner for corner, Julio moved on, until standing alone at the end of the island of Manhattan he looked out on the Hudson River and felt for the first time in a long while the gratitude of the relatively clean, fresh air, skimming off the waters of the river. The breeze cooled his face and hands. He took off the hat and allowed the sweat of his brow to dry in its own time.

To the north, the George Washington Bridge spanned the palisades of the far Jersey shore with the rising slope of Washington Heights. He'd been up this way before, but not for a long time. Washington Heights was Dominican country, a place as foreign to him as the financial district, but far, far more dangerous.

Julio stood unsure of where to go next. Where would he find some wood to make a drum? The whole thing seemed so ridiculous to him now, standing there on the edge of Manhattan, holding the old man's hat and wearing his busted $250 sneakers.

To the north there was only the barren stretch of scrub brush and rails, to the south the riches of the upper west side. Julio felt again the impatience and frustration of his hopeless situation. He kicked a stone that clattered off the indifferent steel of the train tracks.

Julio made his way up the river, following the slender pathway along the train tracks of the northern corridor. He followed the tracks under the hot sun, with the hat providing the only shade.

At one point, Julio grew bored of the straight line of the hardened steel train tracks. He turned into the high grasses of an empty field and with little purpose he wound his way in curious turns through the grasses, until finally he was near the edge of civilization on the western slope.

Julio surveyed his location. He was far from where he'd started that morning. There were some broken down industrial buildings nearby, but otherwise it was desolate.

Julio sat down on an old tire, not knowing what to do, or where to turn next. As he sat he became aware of a sound coming from the old industrial buildings behind him. It was a sound he didn't recognize at first, but one that was familiar in some way to him.

Moving his way carefully through the debris of the abandoned buildings, Julio came closer to the sound. Turning the last corner he spotted a small man feeding long boards into the spinning blade of a table saw. The man wore large, bug-like safety goggles and huge ear mufflers and was completely covered in sawdust. He fed the saw by walking the long boards into the blade, then coming around he grabbed the wood and stacked it neatly on the other side. Julio took the hat off and walked up until he stood just behind the man as he walked the board forward.

The man just caught Julio in the corner of his eye and suddenly turned and stumbled. The board caught on the saw and by the force of its rotation flung it backward with tremendous speed past Julio and the man. With a crash it shattered against the far wall.

Both Julio and the man ducked just in time to avoid the shards of wood that littered the air. When the man stood he ripped off his goggles and ear muffs.

"What the Hell, kid!! You trying to kill me?!" he yelled.

Julio said something, but he was shamed from scaring the man and his voice could not be heard over the saw.

The man leaned over and shut the saw down.

"What?!" he snapped.

"Sorry, I didn't mean to scare you. That was—that—that, was crazy!" stammered Julio.

The little man took a breath, and looking around took note of the shattered board scattered around both of them. He shook his head and began to laugh. But Julio wasn't laughing. After a second, the little man stopped laughing.

"Scram kid, I got work to do." Said the little man as he put his goggles back on.

Julio walked over to the saw, "Hey. Is this wood good for building drums?" he asked, as he picked at the stacked boards. There must have been hundreds of them.

"Drums? I guess so. Don't know much about drums."

Julio ran his hand down the wood and picked up a splinter for his curiosity. He pulled his hand back and began sucking on the splinter.

"Look kid, I'm way behind here." He indicated the uncut boards stacked to the side.

Julio saw the stacks of wood for the first time, "Wow, you got a lot of wood," he said. "So, what are you making?"

The little man was losing the patience he never had, "Tables. Now get lost."

"You think I could have some wood?"

The little man raised the goggles, "Have some?"

"Yea, just a little, for a drum."

He put his goggles back on, "No way."

"Come on, man, look at all this."

"I don't have time to play, kid," said the little man as he picked up another board.

"Wait. I could help you," offered Julio.

The little man thought a second. He looked at the immense stack awaiting him and his solitary efforts.

"My helper just quit, you know."

"Well," said Julio, "now you got me." Julio smiled.

"For how long?"

"As long as it takes, bro. I'll come everyday."

"This isn't a joke, kid. This here's hard work."

"Bring it on."

The little man thought about it again. He liked the look of this kid. He was easily strong enough to handle the work, he decided. But would he show up tomorrow? No way to tell. Either way, he'd get some help out of him right now, and he desperately needed some help if he was going to finish in time.

"My name's Gilbert," said the little man.

"I'm Julio."

"I'll tell you what kid, you help me cut all this wood and I'll give you some. I'll even cut it for you."

"Really?" asked Julio.

"Really," said Gilbert.

"Deal," said Julio, a big grin spreading across his face.

So Gilbert stood on one side of the saw while Julio received and stacked the cut pieces in a nice, neat row. When it came time, Julio reloaded the stack near the saw. It felt good to Julio to have something to do with his hands. Sweat poured off his brow and arms but the smile never left his face. And Gilbert was pleased.

At the garden, night came on in that slow summer way, with the shapeless sky finding its edges by the amber light of the dying sun. Alone, as was his custom, Rafa prepared his evening meal after a long day by the subway entrance with his drums.

Through outside eyes, Rafa's life probably seemed an endless grind of years upon years under heavy, hard impoverished living. But within Rafa's world, one day was no different from the rest. There was only the moment for him, and keeping track of the moments was a labor he'd long ago abandoned in favor of fully experiencing them.

As he cut his food and placed it caringly into the pan, there was only the cutting and the placing. The rice boiled in the small aluminum pan, the lid dancing on the froth, and to Rafa the noise of the dancing lid was not unlike the songs he played on his drums. It was in the moment, alive, and true to its nature. And Rafa, as always, preferred to experience the songs of the moment without interruption from his thoughts and concerns. Even with the boy, Julio, he did not concern himself with his life, only with bringing the world around him into the present.

Almost on cue, Julio came in just as Rafa finished preparing the food. Rafa could tell at once that something good had happened to Julio. His smile was radiant.

"Look what I found," said Julio, too proud to contain himself.

Rafa examined the small piece of wood that Julio handed him.

"This is good wood, mijo!" said Rafa, duly impressed.

"Yea?"

"Gonna be a real small drum, though, you'll have to play it with your pinkies," said Rafa, laughing his belly laugh.

"Man, I got more where that came from, and the man I got it from is going to help me cut it."

"Yea?"

"And he said he might even pay me, so I can help with the food."

"Food?" Rafa checked up, "You moving in or something? I thought you were on your way to Puerto Rico?"

Julio had spoken so quickly and was so excited he'd forgotten to watch what he was saying. In fact, he didn't even realize it was his desire to stay with Rafa until that moment.

"I can go find another place," he said. "You don't have to—"

"I tell you what, mijo," interrupted Rafa, "You can stay until you learn the language of the drum, or until you leave."

Julio smiled, "Sounds cool, I can live with that."

"Let's eat. You can tell me about your day."

And so they ate, and Julio told Rafa all about his day walking the tracks and finding Gilbert and almost killing them both there before he even said a word, and he told him about all the wood piled up and all the cutting and stacking. He told him everything and they laughed and ate and then both of them went to bed well fed and in good company.

CHAPTER 13

During the days that followed, Julio awoke early and dressing in the same shabby clothes and under the cover of the hat Rafa lent him, he walked in the early light down to the place where the wood was being cut. The clothes and the hat, he believed, hid him from the hunting eyes of Santos and his men.

Every morning he left in this way, returning under the shade of nightfall to meet Rafa, back from a day of drumming at the subway entrance, where both shared a simple meal in the garden.

Julio slept inside the casita on the small bed under some blankets Rafa set out for him, while Rafa, preferring his old ways, slept in a hammock hung between the back fence and a sturdy tree.

Finally, the day came. Gilbert, with only a few boards to go, cut the thin slats of wood that would someday become Julio's drum. Gilbert was a good carpenter and given Julio's description and a crude drawing of what the drum was to look like, he cut the wood with uncommon precision.

Then, with a heartfelt handshake, Gilbert handed Julio $300 for the few days work.

"What's this?" demanded Julio.

"You're a good worker, and you got me out of a jam," said Gilbert.

Julio didn't know what to say.

"You earned it. Come back in a month. I'll have more work for you."

"Thanks," said Julio, and he shook Gilbert's hand again.

Julio ran back to Rafa and the Garden with the wood bundle under arm and his hard earned cash tucked tightly in his pocket.

Rafa examined the cutting.

"This is good, mijo. This will build a fine drum," he said.

"He cut it right, just like you drew on the paper, right?" asked Julio.

"It's perfect," answered Rafa.

Julio was proud of himself. It had been so easy to find the wood, so much easier than he ever imagined. He realized that the hardest part of finding the wood had been simply moving beyond his doubts.

Sitting before the freshly cut wood and pride for a job well done, Julio observed the old man and noted how every item he owned, from his drums to his clothes, was old and weathered. Yet they functioned impeccably well, fulfilling a specific purpose and alleviating a need all at the same time. The old man didn't own anything that didn't serve to fill some basic need of his. His life was simple beyond measure.

"Hey Rafa, how long you lived like this?"

"What do you mean?"

"Like, with nothing, man."

"I got everything I need."

"Yea, I know. That's what I mean."

"Well, that aint nothing, mijo."

"You know what I mean."

"No hombre, I don't."

Julio sucked his teeth and shook his head.

"How long you lived in the garden with all your things, man?"

Rafa thought about this for a second.

"A while, I guess. But, where else would I be? This is my place. Those are my drums. I make music on the street for the people who walk it. I eat good every day. That's my hammock where I rest. What else is there, hombre? I don't understand what you ask."

"Forget it, man. It was a stupid question," said Julio.

But Rafa had already gone back to eating and didn't seem to mind or even give it a second thought. He was enjoying the food he'd made, savoring every bite.

When they were done eating, Julio cleared the dishes and washed them in a bucket behind the casita, drying them before returning them to their place. When he finished he came around and found Rafa sitting on the porch examining the wood that would become Julio's drum.

"How much money do I need to finish the drum?"

"You need a little. Not much. You need to buy some glue and ropes and a couple steel rings."

"What kind of drum will it be?"

"A Boku. Very powerful."

"What kind of drums do you play?"

"Those are congas. They speak the language of the streets. They are my eyes, my ears, and my tongue. We are old friends."

"Will the Boku be my eyes and tongue too?"

"The Boku is different. It speaks the language of the ancestors. They will guide you in the beginning of your journey. They will speak in the language of the drum, and it will guide you."

"I thought you were going to teach me."

Rafa laughed. "And who am I? I'm just an old man who lives in a garden eating fried bananas and boiled eggs. The drum is the wise one. Not me." Rafa smiled, "If you want to cook good rice, that's another story."

"Will $50 be enough for the things I need to finish it?"

"Si, plenty. But, you must make a sacrifice. No money can pay for a sacrifice."

"What's that?"

"To give the drum a voice, you make a sacrifice. Before the skin goes on, you make the sacrifice."

"What kind of sacrifice?"

"I'll tell you later. You not ready now."

"I'm ready," said Julio.

"You think you ready. Big difference," said Rafa.

Julio turned red with anger. "You know what old man, you can't tell me nothing about being ready. I'm my own man."

And to prove it, Julio pulled out $100 and tossed it on the porch.

"There's $50 for the drum and $50 for some eggs and rice and whatever else."

Julio began to leave.

"Don't forget your hat," said Rafa.

"It's night."

"Bad things walk the streets at night," was all Rafa said.

Julio reluctantly picked up the old straw hat, and putting it on his head went to the gate and slipped out into the night.

His awareness to the dangers of Santos had become second nature. The shoes, thoroughly broken in by now, were like the silent pads of an alley cat as Julio moved from shadow to shadow in liquid smooth motion. After a few blocks he entered his old neighborhood and with the hat pulled down low on his head became extra careful.

The hairs on his arms tingled. He kept his head down and tried with conscious effort to walk in a way he felt would not betray him to those who might recognize him.

As he kept his head down he recognized the shambles of his wardrobe, with the busted sneakers and the faded unfashionable jeans and the worn dusty dress shirt from the woodpile. He looked like a bum, and not just any bum, a broken down bum.

Shame rose up from within him—shame for the way in which he was returning to his neighborhood. But he moved on, determined, with each step inevitably brining the danger of Santos closer.

When he turned the corner, his heart stopped.

Oscar and Tony were coming up the block.

If Oscar hadn't been looking Tony's way and Tony hadn't been talking, they would have seen Julio for sure. But both the men were in a heated discussion, at least Tony's side was loud and livid.

Julio didn't have time for anything. Running meant drawing attention. He had a moment to make a decision, so he threw himself down between the garbage bags and pulled the hat down low, pretending he was just another junkie, strung out on the streets.

Using the hat as a shield, he could just barely see through the loose straw of the brim, as if peering past the tight corners of a keyhole. The light from the street lamp came through, making foggy stars in Julio's eyes.

Off to the side he could hear them coming. He could hear Tony's voice raising and hear the words pouring from his mouth as he came on.

"This thing's out of control, man! We gettin robbed every damn day. They making fools out of us! We don't stop this and Santos gonna kill us."

When the two came even with Julio, Tony was still talking, but Oscar, ever aware, turned, and catching Julio's discarded body there amongst the trash slowed to a stop.

Julio could see Oscar staring down on him. Oscar took a step forward, his hand moving up towards the inside of his jacket. Julio's heart was going mad in his chest, beating like a bird's. Tony finally turned, some paces beyond Oscar, and seeing his partner had stopped, put his arms up in protest.

"Hey, I'm talking to you man, can't you even listen to me?"

Oscar took another step forward and with a quick glance to either side, eased the gun from his jacket.

Tony came alive.

"What the hell you doing?" he demanded as he went for his own gun.

It was too much for Julio, he wanted to run, but he couldn't will himself to rise. With all his effort he demanded his legs to move, commanding himself to flee, but no movement came. He was frozen to the floor. Like a wounded animal he waited for Oscar to finish him off.

Suddenly, the peering in Oscar pulled back, and putting the gun away stopped the advancing Tony with a stiff halting hand to the chest. Oscar turned and began walking again down the block as if nothing had even happened.

"What the hell was that?" said Tony, standing with his gun pulled between the departing Oscar and Julio.

Tony was reluctant to let it go. He looked down at Julio in the hat, his body as motionless between the dirty bags of garbage as the bags themselves. But his look was without the intensity or interest of Oscar's, and in a moment he was gone.

"You crazy ass, you trying to give me a heart attack?" said Tony, putting his own gun away and following Oscar down the block.

Julio took a breath for what seemed like the first time in his life. It tasted strong of garbage. Gently he turned his head to peer from under the hat at the diminishing backs of Oscar and Tony.

Just as his eyes cleared a line of sight between them, Oscar turned back with a sharp glance. But Julio played it cool and with imperceptible ease lowered the brim of the hat until he was sure the two were long gone.

Then he picked himself up out of the garbage and walked on, moving with even more stealth and care than before. His nerves frayed from the sense that all the evil in the world could come crashing down on him at any moment.

Finally, he came to his aunt's building and waiting for the right moment. As a neighbor of his aunt entered, Julio slipped in behind before the door locked closed, and with silent strides, Julio scaled the steps leading up to his aunt's floor.

At the door he knocked, at first timidly, but when she didn't answer he became panicked that she wouldn't be there at all. He needed her to be home right now. She was always home at this time.

He knocked harder. Finally he heard something moving.

"Tia!" he whisper shouted.

"Tia!"

"Tia! It's me, Julio."

"Let me in!"

The bolt lock clicked open followed by the bottom lock and finally the door cracked open, stopping short on the chain. Sylvia stood on the other side, her face framed by the cracked doorway. She looked exhausted.

"What do you want?"

"Tia, let me in. Please. I have something for you."

Without a word she shut the door.

Julio wanted to cry.

Then she opened it again, this time without the chain and with the wide swing of the door Julio's heart followed.

Taking a seat in the kitchen, she waited for Julio to come in on soft feet with eyes lowered until he took his seat at the far end of the table. It was strange for Julio to be in the kitchen again. It seemed so long ago that he'd had fought with his tia and had left for what he believed would be the last time. It was so much smaller than memory, the smells so much stronger, and his aunt so much older and frailer than he'd remembered. Everything had changed, he realized. Yet everything remained the same.

"So, what do you want?" she said with her hands idle, resting on her lap beneath the table.

"I've been working, tia. I found a place to work."

"I'm sure you have."

"I helped a man cut some wood down by the river. He paid me good."

Sylvia said nothing. She only stared at Julio in her kitchen.

"He's a really strange guy. Real nice to me," continued Julio.

Julio with one hand toyed with the money in his pocket.

"We just finished with the one project. He says he'll have more work for me soon."

Julio waited, but there was nothing to wait for. His aunt sat silent as before. Non-believing. Waiting. Watching.

Julio stayed with his pocket.

"I wanted to give you some money," he said, and pulled out a wadded up bundle of cash—the remaining $200, "I want to help with the rent, you know. I wanted to—"

But Sylvia cut him off.

"Your friends came looking for you."

"My friends?" he put the money down on the table.

"You know, the guy with the scar and that awful Italian guy."

"They came here?"

"They were here."

"What did they say?"

"What do you think they said?" she asked, impatient.

Julio swallowed hard.

"I don't know."

"They're looking for you."

"Did they hurt you?"

Sylvia took a breath. "No," she replied, "not this time."

Julio was relieved. "What'd they say?" he asked again.

"They're drug dealers, aren't they?"

"Why do you always think everyone is a drug dealer?"

Sylvia slammed her palm on the table with deafening force. With the blow she came forward in her chair, her finger up, accusing, and behind a fire lit in her eyes.

"You think I'm so stupid, don't you?"

"I didn't say they weren't."

She sat back, but the fire remained.

"That's a neat trick," she said, "I know. You owe them some money or something and now you want to give me your dirty drug money. Why? So when they come to kill me and my children I can try and stop them. With your dirty money? You're so thoughtful."

"Tia, I worked for this money." Julio wanted so much for her to understand, "I want to help you."

She stood there silent as a loaded gun.

Julio squirmed, and then said the only thing on his mind, "I'm building a drum."

"A drum?!" for the moment he had actually shocked her. "You know what, you're crazy," she said shaking her head. But, then the anger came, "You're living on the streets. You think I'm so stupid! You're a bum! Look at your clothes. Look at you! You are nothing but a loser and a drug dealer. You're poison to everything you touch."

Julio felt his insides crumbling. His heart was breaking before her in her kitchen. If she would have put a knife into him it would have been a hundred times less painful.

"Tia, don't say that. It isn't true, tia."

"Get out! Get out of my sight," her fingers, strong and lean from all the years of labor pointed at the doorway, "Don't ever come here again. If you do, I'll call the police."

"No tia, please," pleaded Julio.

"Get out, I said! Get out of here!"

She stood and with all the fire in her eyes and hands came at him, but he jumped up and with tears beginning to stream went to the door. When he got there he turned and Sylvia spotting the cash on the table reached over and grabbed it.

"No tia, please," he pleaded with her, "that's for you. I worked for it, to help you, I promise."

She grabbed his hand and stuffed the cash into it.

"I don't need you and I don't want your dirty drug money!"

Then she pushed him out the door and slammed it shut.

Julio stood facing the door a moment, the cold flat surface only inches from his face. He became aware of the money clenched in his hand. Rejection rained down on him and soaked his spirit through. Finally, he turned and walked down the hallway. When he reached the stairs he met his little cousins at the top of the stairwell. They were out of breath.

Mariela, the oldest, said nothing. She just glared at Julio as she ushered Monica and Miguel past. Julio's fist trembled, loosely clutching the cash, his mind whirling with thoughts of what to do. He thought of giving Mariela the cash. He wanted to tell her to hide it and give it to her mother at the right moment. He wanted to tell her to help with the rent and the food. He wanted her to help him. But she just stared with bitter eyes that held him in contempt, as if he were a dangerous and irrational criminal.

He held the money and his tongue, until he finally failed to hold even her eyes. Turning at once, he descended the stairs and disappeared from their lives forever.

CHAPTER 14

Rafa sat beneath the shelter of the roof, his chair leaning against the casita. Above, the stars hid behind the dim soapy sky, washed clean by the haze of city lights. The wind came in soft, suggesting the ease of a cloudless summer night.

Rafa's features were shadows on shadows in the shadows of the eve. With the darkness of the little house falling about him and taking him in, he became only a shade of grey on one of its many sides.

From beyond the gate, Julio came in silently, slipping with quick backward glances into the shadows held by the garden fence. His shoulders were tight from the near tragic meeting with Oscar and the failure at his aunt's house. He knew now that Oscar was on to him and he knew from the legends of the street that when Oscar was on the hunt, you were as good as dead.

The knowledge that he'd brought his aunt into the whole mess made Julio sink beneath the lowest branches of his mind. With all this pressing despair, Julio stepped into the garden. As he did, he felt a subtle calming presence, as the coolness of the foliage thick air took him in.

Passing the casita a voice came from the shadows.

"The anger she feels is just concern for you," said the voice.

Julio froze, his heart suddenly leaping in great thumps in his chest. He stood a moment in the darkness hoping to find Rafa's eyes, but the shadows held their grip.

"What?" asked Julio finally, but he knew. The question he really wanted to ask was, *how do you know I went to see her*?

But to ask that would imply that Rafa somehow knew, and that idea scared him.

"She loves you, Julio," said Rafa, as his chair came down with a creak onto the deck.

Julio stood quiet for a moment.

"How do you know?"

"Bah! I know because beneath everything there is love, and only love. She just scared."

Julio located the old man in the shadows and his heart calmed to see the familiar lines of his face and the ever-present smile.

"I'm scared, too," said Julio and it was the first time in his life he'd admitted that to anyone. The first time he'd even admitted it to himself.

"Good," said Rafa. "You beginning to wake up."

But Julio didn't feel like he was waking up, and if he was, it was waking from a nightmare that only became more real with the waking. With the money an uncomfortable bulk in his pocket, Julio found his corner in the casita and within a few moments fell into a fitful sleep.

The old man Rafa smiled to himself, sitting on the chair in the shadows. With practiced ease Rafa lost himself amongst the stars of the night sky once again. His eyes again closed down and turned inward as a gentle smile formed effortlessly on his lips. He felt himself dissolve and the garden come up to fill him until he could not distinguish where he himself ended and the garden began.

He felt himself take a deep breath and with the breath he relaxed further and felt more of the world join together harmoniously and he himself somewhere within, as if his consciousness were filling out the sky. It felt as if he were rising on air, gently, effortlessly, on wings made of silken feathers. Just as the casita disappeared below him he saw a man he didn't know crouched outside the gates of the garden, surrounded in the shadows of evil intention, with his eyes looking in.

CHAPTER 15

After Rafa returned from his morning session at the subway stop, it took only the early afternoon for he and Julio, working side by side, to complete the gluing of the drum. After the glue was set, Julio and Rafa admired the bound wooden slats forming the familiar shape of the Boku drum.

The wood was marvelously cut. Even Julio, who had never before built a drum or anything else in his life, could tell that there was power and magic at work within the binding elements of the drum. He danced around it pretending to play the imaginary skin that someday would become real. He made noises with his mouth imitating the rhythms Rafa had played for him.

"This is going to be a good drum. I can feel it!"

"Si mijo, you have good senses." said Rafa. "Si indeed."

Rafa came and covered the drum with a thin scarf adorned with the colors of the Puerto Rican flag. It was worn from years of good use.

"Let's give her some privacy," said Rafa. "So she can find her parts and make them whole."

All the mysticism was new and strange to Julio. He'd been to church a few times with his tia, and he prayed to God when he was expected to, and believed in God when it made sense to him. But, to see Rafa, who never went to church, or even spoke of God, to have constant awareness of something beyond, made Julio think that perhaps there was something more out there that he'd missed.

Maybe he's a wizard, thought Julio, or maybe he's just crazy. All Julio knew was that when Rafa played the drums, the drums themselves spoke to him. He wasn't sure if it was Rafa speaking to him from behind the drums or not, but he knew from the depths of his heart that what he learned from the drums was the voice of some kind of God that knew him well—too well, in fact, to be Rafa.

It was a voice that wanted him to be happy and free. It was a voice that guided him. More than anything, he wanted his own drum so that he could connect himself with the voice every day.

When the drum was covered, Rafa stood and suddenly became aware of something new in the air. He turned to Julio with building tension in his voice.

"Now would be a good time to buy the supplies for the drum."

"What's next?"

"You need the rings and the rope. You will find these things with a man named Nacho. He's at the end of 125th, near the Harlem River."

"You're not coming?"

"I have something else to do."

Rafa spoke quickly with a snap to his words. He was acting strange, thought Julio, as if he knew something that he wasn't going to explain. More than that, Julio could sense that he should leave the garden at once. He didn't know from where the feeling came, or for what reason, he only knew that it was present.

Rafa quickly wrote with delicate script a short list of instructions on a ragged slip of paper. He measured the circumference of the drum with his outstretched fingers and added the information. He handed the slip of paper to Julio.

"Use the money you left me. It's in the drawer there. Nacho will give you everything you need. You will find him in the factory by the water, sitting in his office, doing nothing."

"How much do I need?"

"Take it all with you. There's no way to tell what might happen."

Julio went to the drawer. He found all but the few dollars they'd spent on the glue and the binding ropes. Rafa had taken no money for food. Julio wanted to tell him to take the money and buy food for them. But, now didn't seem the time to bring it up, so he bundled the cash and stuffed it into his pocket with the rest of his money from the job, then he put on the hat and the dusted work shirt. Rafa waited on the porch and watched Julio go out the garden gate.

He said nothing to the boy as he left.

Sure that Julio was gone, the concern that had turned Rafa's mouth and eyes sour relaxed a bit. Rafa sat alone now with the sense that a powerful evil was closing in on them. He only hoped that Julio had gone far enough so that if he could not contain what was to come, then Julio would have enough of a head start to get free.

The sense of imminent danger became a raging storm within him; deafening beyond control. It seemed to fill the sky so that not even the birds could find space to fly. It came on relentless, until suddenly all that had been poison inside broke, leaving him afloat on a profound sense of calm and crystalline clarity.

And now he comes, thought Rafa.

Julio hit the street and pulling the hat down low, disappeared quickly into the growing foot traffic on the sidewalk. He dipped between the cars and down the rubbish-strewn alleyways; his senses keen to imminent dangers. For weeks he'd been living with the risk of Santos and his men breathing down his neck, and the fugitive way had become like second nature to him.

Only once he hit 125th did Julio allow himself to relax a bit. The crowd swelled up around him, coating him with its chatter as the honking, squelching and squeaking automobile street traffic threatened to drown them all. Submersed in the hustle of 125th it would be harder to see Santos or his men approaching, but then again, thought Julio, he would be harder to spot as well. Not to mention the well known fact that Santos and his men avoided crowded areas, preferring the backs of deserted restaurants or otherwise private areas for their daily business.

When Santos came out into public it was for a reason and that reason would never be running around looking for a kid, unless he were coming out to pull the trigger himself. To be constantly hunting and searching and failing to find Julio would indicate a weakness. By the same token, Julio knew that Santos would only tolerate not being able to find him for so long. Then he would come with all guns blazing in a shakedown search and destroy mission. Julio knew that even now perhaps Santos had had enough. That moment could come at any time.

But on 125th in the afternoon with the sun shining and the people crowding the streets, that outcome seemed far removed from Julio's reality. Even still, he moved quickly through the crowd and avoided all eye contact. He pulled the hat low, setting his stride quick and secure. He looked like any other rush on the streets of New York, and his clothes were far from flashy, or even remotely like anything anyone his age would wear. Pretty girls walked by and paid him no mind, and even though he wished he could stop and talk with them, he felt the stakes were too high.

As he weaved his way down 125th, he thought of how much had changed in the last few weeks, and how at times his old life was completely dead to him. He thought back on the shoes when they were new and how he'd coveted their promises in his room that morning. He looked down and saw them broken and worn, unable to connect with their obvious comfort at all.

It depressed him, so Julio thought of the old man.

Rafa had become a good friend, his only friend in fact, and in many ways the only true friend he'd ever had. These days, Julio thought about the drum constantly, the drum and the rhythms that would show him the secrets within himself.

But in a moment all that was gone too.

Julio felt a prideful anger wash over him. It wanted him to go buy a gun and hunt down Santos before Santos could hunt him down. He wanted to defend himself. He wanted to find Santos and Oscar and Tony, and kill them all.

Why, he bet, if he killed off Santos, Oscar and Tony would probably turn their allegiances over to him. Then Julio would become the biggest, baddest gangster in the hood. He could get that car and the girls, and he could buy all the drums he wanted. He could play the drums and the girls could do a strip tease for him. Julio liked that idea.

A smile cut across his face from under the hat—and just like that, his strut hit stride.

It felt good to feel the bounce again. Been too long, he thought. A part of him came alive, a part he had been missing. He even allowed his head to come up a bit so that beneath the hat he could see down the street. As he walked, he started to count off all the suckers he came across and in a moment felt he was badder than anyone on the streets.

Two girls came strolling down 125th with their summer whites and bright smiles and Julio, in only the way he could, tipped his hat and flashed a big grin.

"Hey ladies," he said with the seduction smile.

They giggled and smiled back and Julio just kept on.

He still had it.

He wanted this life back. It was as if from within this part of him had tired of hiding, and now it was time to come true. If only he could get his hands on a gun, he thought. If only! Then he could find Santos and sneak in and kill him. He wouldn't shoot Santos in the back. He'd say, 'Hey, I heard you were looking for me.' Then he'd wait for Santos to go for his gun, and before Santos could fire a shot, he'd gun him down looking straight into his eyes. Pow! Pow! Two shots—one to the heart, one to the head. It would be that easy. Santos wouldn't know what hit him. Then, seeing that their leader was dead, both Oscar and Tony would turn over their loyalties and Julio would have his run of the streets. It was too easy, Julio decided. Why hadn't he thought of it before?

Julio looked up and recognized the old buildings of the far eastern side of 125th. He remembered Slow Eddie's pawn shop just around the corner and feeling the over $250 in his pocket, veered north off 125th towards Slow Eddie's.

CHAPTER 16

Rafa sat on the porch waiting. He knew not what was about to come, but he knew it was evil beyond measure. He waited, and with him the garden shared its patience.

At that very moment, Oscar turned into the gates of the garden. He walked with his hands in his pockets, as if out for a weekend stroll. Although he held his head high, his eyes were down, watching from low angles the garden as it unfolded before him. He walked as if he'd been this way before; as he did everywhere he went.

He strolled forward, until he stood before Rafa sitting in the chair on the porch. A moment passed with both men silent, and still—watching. Oscar casually turned a toothpick over in his mouth.

Rafa, his body frail and weathered, sat calmly before him and before the faded colors of the once brightly painted porch. When he looked into Oscar's eyes he felt as if a cold and empty wind had blown across his heart.

Oscar took the creaking steps of the casita and went to Julio's drum. With delicate fingers took the corner of the old fabric covering the drum and lifted it. He held it high enough to see the newly constructed drum. When he had seen enough, he nodded knowingly, impressed. Rafa watched him.

Suddenly Oscar looked up and locked eyes with Rafa and although Rafa was at the ready, he was not prepared for the power of Oscar's gaze. Oscar smiled. This time he had seen what he was looking for. The old man had given him what he wanted to know. Oscar took his eyes back to the garden.

It pleased him to be in the garden.

With the ease of a Sunday afternoon, Oscar took a seat on the porch. He shifted a bit, as a man preparing for a nap in a hammock might, coming to a more comfortable, more relaxed position with his back against the post. He let his head come back to rest as he tooled the toothpick between his teeth. It was a pleasant afternoon.

Oscar took a deep breath, then flicked his arm up with such speed it seemed to blur across the eye and in an instant he held his gun at the ready. His jacket had barely even moved. With hypnotic ease and precision he twirled the gun around his finger, snapping the gun into his palm. He did it again, and again. The move was near silent, quick, and menacing. The gun was like a nimble extension of Oscar's arm.

He looked up at Rafa, who stared at him from his seat on the porch. Oscar, still smiling, still relaxed, still enjoying the garden, with even more blinding speed brought the gun up and held the space between Rafa's eyes between the sights.

He waited a moment, then "Pow," he mouthed with silent lips, feigning the requisite kick of a fired shell. His smile faded, and Rafa saw the anger and greed manifest in Oscar's eyes, as if the fires of Hell were themselves lit by his gaze.

Oscar's smile returned, bringing with it a calm and seductive charm. Again, he was just a simple man enjoying the garden. Just as smooth as it had come out, Oscar put the gun away. He rose from the porch and plucked a flower from a nearby plant, sniffing it pensively as he walked as slowly and confidently as he'd come. He paused a moment at the gate, then without looking back, walked out of the garden and into the street.

CHAPTER 17

When Julio made the shop window he stopped and looked in. He saw Eddie was there. Eddie was always there, sitting behind the dusty counter top beneath the same collection of guitars and hubcaps that had hung from the rafters ever since Julio first stepped into the spot. Eddie poked a plastic fork into a pile of cold Chinese food as he read the newspaper.

Julio hopped that Eddie wouldn't recognize him. It had been a long time since Julio had been in Eddie's shop, perhaps Eddie wouldn't even remember. Julio tossed the hat and the dusty shirt behind the dumpster by the door and went in. The overhead bell rang. Eddie instinctively looked up from his food. He considered Julio with less than cursory glance, and then returned to his food.

Good, thought Julio, he didn't recognize me.

Julio wound his way around the stale goods, pretending to be interested in this and that. He aimlessly thumbed his way through some old records, before moving on to a barrel containing umbrellas, golf clubs, canes and a fishing rod. He pulled out the fishing rod and whipped it around a little to test the tensile. It swipped and swished through the air.

Fast Eddie stubbed the fork in the pile of food and looked up. He wasn't a patient man, and he wasn't running a toy store.

"Hey kid!" shouted Eddie, "What gives?!"

Julio dropped the rod back in the can then came over to the counter. Eddie sat there with an elbow on the counter.

"I need a piece."

"Yea right," said Eddie, going back to his food. With a fresh mouthful he added, "You think I'm selling *you* a piece? You're nuts."

Julio took out the $200 and waved it at Eddie. Eddie stopped chewing.

"How much?" he grumbled.

"Two hundred."

"Two hundred?"

"Two hundred," said Julio, again.

Eddie wiped his mouth with the back of his hand. He chewed his food with his eyes moving from the money, to Julio, and back to the money. He pushed back from the counter and reaching into a drawer at his knees came up holding a slick, all black .38 caliber revolver. He weighed it a moment in his hand, then tossed it onto the counter in front of Julio.

It came down with a heavy thump.

As Julio's hand came up to take the gun, Eddie came down hard and grabbed Julio's wrist. Eddie was strong and quick—much stronger and quicker than Julio ever imagined.

With a crushing grip Eddie twisted and yanked Julio in close, slamming his body against the counter so that Julio could smell the cheap Chinese grease on Eddie's mustache.

"You tell anyone where you got this thing, and kid—you'll wish you'd never been born. You hear me?" he said pulling up hard on Julio's wrist.

Dust floated in the air between them. Julio's feet were off the ground, clamoring to find a step at the base of the counter.

Julio fought to get the words out from behind the clenching of his jaw.

"Yea, I got it," he finally said through pursed lips.

"What?"

"I got it! I said, I got it!"

Eddie let go the wrist and Julio fell back from the counter. With one hand he covered the gun and raised the open palm of the other towards the money.

Julio hesitated and rubbed his burning wrist.

"How do I know it works?"

"If it don't work, bring it back," said Eddie, then he laughed.

And Julio saw his moment, because when Eddie laughed he took his hand off the gun just enough so that Julio grabbed it—too quick for Eddie to stop him. As Julio stepped back, he cocked the hammer and then came forward until the point of the snub nosed barrel rested right in Eddie's face.

"Save myself a little time if I test it out right now," he said, cool as ice. "Don't you think?"

Eddie went white, his jaw dropping and shaking, "It works, kid. I swear," he struggled to swallow. "You don't wanna do that."

"Oh," said Julio, adjusting his grip on the gun, "I want to, believe me."

Julio held the gun there, his finger pressing down on the smooth face of the trigger. He liked the feeling of power he had over Eddie. After all the days of running scared, he felt reborn.

Sweat began to trickle down Eddie's brow, causing Julio to smile.

"Man, I want to pull this trigger in the worst way."

Julio waited, playing with Eddie's nerves. Then he pulled back the gun and began to examine it. He was a kid again, giddy with his new toy.

"I guess it's loaded, eh," he said, tossing the two hundred on the counter. Julio checked the chamber and pulled out a couple of the shells to verify what he already knew. The gun was fully loaded. A smile came to his face as he jammed the gun under his belt at the small of his back.

With money in hand, the color quickly returned to Eddie's face, even passing red in the aftermath. Julio knew Eddie wanted to say something, but to say more might cause someone to get shot, and Eddie had it too good to spoil it shooting kids or getting shot himself before he could finish his lunch.

Julio turned to leave.

"Hey," snapped Eddie.

Julio turned.

"You better be careful who you point that thing at, some guys weren't meant to die."

A cold fear ran up Julio's spine, and then it was gone.

"What does that mean?" asked Julio.

"Means what it means. Remember kid, you didn't get that thing from me."

Julio smiled again.

"Don't worry, aint nobody gonna be left to ask."

Outside the shop and Eddie's line of sight, Julio put on the work shirt and the hat disguise and walked toward the factory Rafa had sent him to find. He felt better now that he had the gun. As he walked he thought about what he would say to Santos just before he shot him dead.

CHAPTER 18

Rafa sat on the porch with the calm inside of him bathing him with reassurance. There was no moment with Oscar in which Rafa felt abandoned by his inner rhythm—a thing he called his clave—or threatened by fear.

It would be easy to say that an old man like Rafa, so wise and well lived, was a man who no longer feared death, as each day death became more and more likely with the inevitable passing of time. But this wouldn't be true for Rafa. He simply followed the guidance of his clave, and where it took him was where it took him. His faith in the wisdom of the drum was unbending, so that if Oscar had come to kill him, and his clave would not have prevented it in some way, then it was as meant to be as the rising of the morning sun.

After Oscar and his dangers left, Rafa set into preparing lunch for himself and Julio. He prepared the food as always, taking care, moving slowly, with precision, and keeping his absolute focus on the task at hand. Just as Rafa finished cleaning up the cookware, Julio walked in carrying the supplies in a large plastic bag.

Immediately, Rafa sensed the change in Julio. The walk was different. His hat was laid back and there was a certain pop of confidence and defiance to his walk.

Rafa shook his head, "What took you so long?" he asked.

The response was instantaneous.

"Damn, dude! You my old lady or something?"

He threw the bag down on the porch for effect, spilling the contents across the thin boards.

Julio spat at the ground.

Rafa stood beside the freshly cleaned pots drying his hands with a towel. He surveyed the rings and the rope, seeing everything there that was needed for the drum. Julio had done what he'd asked. But Rafa could feel the money sickness in Julio again. Dark shadows followed Julio as he paced around the front of the casita, shadows familiar to Rafa, the same shadows he'd seen with the coming of Oscar.

"Looks like you found more than rings," said Rafa.

Julio stopped dead.

"What's that supposed to mean?" he answered.

Rafa waited patiently. Julio began to feel a little uncomfortable.

"What do you want from me, old man?" he demanded.

"Only that you listen to yourself."

"I hear just fine, viejo."

"You think so?"

"Yea!"

Rafa nodded. "Ok, hotshot. Then listen to this, I saw your friend today, the one with the scar, the one who doesn't speak. He came here. He knows you're here."

Julio could barely get the word past his lips.

"What?"

Rafa smiled. "I thought you said you were listening."

"He came here?"

Rafa shook his head and sucked at his teeth. He spoke slow and clear, "You don't hear so good, kid. I said he was here, and he knows you here," repeated Rafa.

"You told him?"

Rafa gave Julio a look. "He's powerful, powerful enough to know."

"What does that mean?"

"I can only protect you if you stay close. Go too far, and he kill you," said Rafa, matter of fact.

Julio folded his arms.

"I don't need your protection, old man. I can take care of myself."

"How? With that little gun you got in your back pocket?"

Julio's arms came down.

"What are you talking about?"

Rafa threw his arms up, "Damn kid, you deaf! You don't hear nothing!" said Rafa.

"I heard you!" Julio blasted. Rafa's word games made him so mad sometimes. Instinctively, he put his hand behind him.

"How did you know about the gun?" he asked.

"The same way I knew he was coming. The same way I know you. The same way I know you got money sickness. And, the same way I know he'll kill you dead, even if you have that little gun. I speak the language of the drum, mijo, and she tells me everything."

Julio hesitated.

"I was going to kill his boss, so that he would leave us alone," he admitted.

Rafa shook his head.

"Well, I don't know nothing about his boss. But this guy—no way Jose! This guy who come today, he kill you for sure."

"What do I do?"

"Stay close, kid. I can protect you, but only if you stay close."

"How you gonna protect me?"

"You'll see, nothing will happen if you stay close to me."

Julio didn't know what to say. The cruel reality was that he knew Oscar was deadly. More deadly than anyone he'd ever heard of—other than Santos, that is. He had no choice but to listen to the old man.

"O.K." said Julio, "I'll be cool. I'll do what you say."

Rafa only nodded, but wasted no time.

"Give me the gun."

Julio hesitated.

"Give it to me, now." demanded Rafa, and Julio did as he was told.

Rafa held the gun in his hand with the same intent one might hold a cold stone. He quickly turned and disappeared into the casita, closing the door behind him.

But the door didn't latch. Not completely, and in a moment it silently crept open.

Julio hesitated a moment, then quickly and quietly moved so that he could peer inside as Rafa removed the worn rug on the floor and reveald the thin outline of a trap door. Rafa opened it and unceremoniously dropped the pistol inside and closing the trap door returned the rug to its eternal resting place.

Julio quickly stepped back away from the casita as if he'd seen none of it.

Rafa came out and pointed, "From now on, you leave the garden out the back, and come in that way too. I'll show you the way."

Julio looked down the dark path that began under the bent opening of the back fence. The grass was high and if Rafa hadn't pointed it out, Julio wouldn't have seen the path at all. From the opening, Julio could see that the path led a narrow line down the back of all the buildings on the block. He would be able to enter and leave the garden from a number of points.

"All paths lead to the street, except one. If you go carefully, nobody will ever know when you come or go."

"Where does the one go?"

"When you find it, you'll know."

"What does that mean?" Julio could feel the anger rising again.

"It means, what it means, mijo," said Rafa, and he smiled. "Listen, he gone now. Relax. Let's look at those things you bring."

Julio followed Rafa over to where the discarded bag lay open with its contents spewed. Rafa dumped out the rest of the bag then picked up the elements of the drum and organized them into little piles.

There was a coil of rope, like the kind mountain climbers use, except thinner, it was very strong and smooth to the touch. There were three steel rings, two of same size—only slightly larger than the opening at the top of the drum—and another smaller ring that would arrest itself near the middle of the drum.

Alongside these necessary components lay a package of sandpaper, a small bottle of linseed oil and some rags.

"Looks good, kid. Looks real good! You got everything you need," said Rafa.

Julio brightened, he was getting excited again.

"Except the skin," Julio added.

"Si, the skin," agreed Rafa.

Julio was relieved he wasn't carrying the gun anymore. It seemed strange to him that in one moment he could be so ready and willing to kill and fight for the power and influence of the streets and in the next he was interested in only the drum and his inner rhythm. He felt as if he were split in two.

He was happy that Rafa was there to help protect him from Oscar. The truth was, Oscar would kill him if he found him. Julio knew that. He also knew that alone he would never be able to stop him.

CHAPTER 19

By the next afternoon the glue had dried on Julio's new drum and after returning from his morning at play before the subway entrance, Rafa showed Julio how to sand the drum using the sandpaper, moving it in the direction of the wood-grain. It was hard, dusty work, and as Julio labored in the shade of the old tree, Rafa sat comfortably on the porch playing his drums. In this way Julio was able to find a groove in which to work. He bopped along to the rhythms of Rafa's drumming and when he could, he added to the sweet sounds with the shooka-shacka-scratch of the paper across the wood.

After a few hours, Julio finished. The whole while he labored on the drum it had seemed more like play than work. Julio was tired, but the wood of the drum was smooth, showing no lines from where the boards had come together with the help of the glue. It had a soft, smooth look to it, as if you were looking at it off the reflection of a still lake on a foggy morning. The lip where the skin would eventually rest was sanded down and made so that when struck with the hands it caused no discomfort. Julio took extra care, even popping his palms off the raw wood in order to test it so that he was sure it was right for him. Rafa had instructed him to do this, and Julio had with great patience and care followed his instruction.

Once the sanding was done, Julio cleaned off the body of the drum with a wet rag and applied a smooth coat of linseed oil for a finish. The wood took the oils in its thirsty pores, and as the oils soaked in, the wood emitted a luster and shimmering depth that belied the realities of its solid flat surface.

By the evening, in the magical light of the setting sun, Julio stood on the ground with his newly polished drum seated like royalty on the edge of the porch.

As Julio had been building, Rafa had been playing the entire way, stopping only to give advice and answer questions. Unbeknown to Julio, Rafa had played the rhythms of his ancestors, tracking back the Puerto Ricans who were at one time Africans and Spaniards who carried their rhythms with them along side their souls, and back still further before them to the Arawak Indians with their drums and spirit worlds living out their simple lives under care of the Caribbean sun. Without knowing, Julio had been given full and varied exposure to the history of rhythm of his people.

The drum had come out nearly perfect. The wood was good wood indeed. It was a drum that if properly cared for would last Julio a lifetime. Rafa stood at his side, the two of them admiring the day's work. The drum practically glowed, held gently alight by the fading light of the setting sun.

Suddenly, Julio grabbed Rafa and gave him a strong hug. It only lasted a moment before Julio pulled away, too proud to make it stick. But, it had happened, and for both of them it was a great moment.

CHAPTER 20

The next day Julio awoke and coming from the casita found, as he always did, Rafa waiting with a steaming plate of rice, boiled eggs, and sweet plantains.

"Man, you weren't joking," said Julio, "You eat that stuff every damn day."

"It's all a man needs."

"If you're trying to turn into a banana," said Julio with much sarcasm. Rafa laughed.

"You talk now, but wait until later, you be thanking me."

"What's today, anyway?" asked Julio.

"Today we get the skin."

"Where?"

"We go to a special place. Es una Botanica. El Congo Real. There we will get the skin. They have the right skins."

Julio knew that place. He'd never been in there, but it was talked about by many in the community who went there seeking the oils, perfumes, candles and figurines of traditional Hispanic spiritual medicine. One could even have their fortune read in the back. It had always been a foreign place to Julio. Every time he'd pass by there were only the older men and women of the community awaiting service. For Julio, the place was a dying relic. His aunt had been there a few times to buy candles, which she used when seeking help during troubled times. But from Julio's perspective, trouble had a way of getting past all that anyway.

"Aint that one of those Santería voodoo spots?"

Rafa nodded, "You can find that there, if that is what you seek," he said. "Everything you find depends on what you seek."

Julio nodded his head.

Both ate their breakfast in silence. Both chewed their food with conscious care, making sure to take time to enjoy the process of nourishing their bodies. For Julio, this was a new thing, for he'd always eaten in a tremendous rush. There was always some place to be.

Sylvia had tried to get him to enjoy his food, but somehow being in her kitchen and under her watchful eyes made him rush all the more. With Rafa, however, he felt as if there were never any rush. They did what they did, and then they moved on to what was next, never rushing, never sacrificing care for speed, never compromising quality of experience for instant gratification, never moving on to what was next until what was now was finished. Julio learned all this with Rafa, and Rafa had never said a word of instruction about it. He just lived it, and by proximity, so learned Julio.

The food was good, it was always good. And more than that it was the kind of food that for some reason didn't make Julio tired, he always felt energized and well fueled for the day. When Julio finished, he did the dishes in the sink. He was silent, and had been for some time. Finally he found Rafa's eyes.

"What about Oscar?" he asked.

"You mean the man who wants to kill you?"

Julio didn't like the sound of that, "Yea, that guy."

Rafa nodded, he understood.

"Come, sit down," said Rafa, "sit close."

Julio sat near the drums.

"Close your eyes," he said, and Julio did.

Rafa went to his drums. After a few deep breaths, he began playing, sending his rhythms out into the world. But there was something else to his playing. Something that Julio hadn't heard before. It was like the finger of a beautiful woman waving him in. Julio relaxed and found himself being taken into the sound of the drums, as if his head were cradled between her gentle hands.

The sound was everywhere, all around him. He felt dizzy, as if the world suddenly had no bottom and no top. He fought the urge to open his eyes, he fought the urge to panic, and he fought to stay focused on the gentle beaconing of the rhythms. He relaxed, finally, and in a gentle rush the rhythms took him in.

Julio felt himself sailing on the winds, a guest of the waves of rhythm that surrounded him. He felt himself go lightly into the air. Below, the blocks gently materialized for him, not so much in sight as one might see with their eyes, but in feeling, as one lying in bed with eyes closed might perceive the boundaries of their room. It was as if he were standing on a pole hundreds of feet above the garden. He could feel the city below him in all its summer charm. He could feel the playfulness of the streets and the innocence of all the people that populated it.

Then, with increasing perception, another force called to him, coming far off to the East. At once Julio recognized it as the barbershop where Santos hung out. He could feel a darkness and impatience coming from there. He could feel the shadows spreading out like spokes on a wheel, turning and grinding the air like a death machine. A shiver of darkness like a brittle cold wave passed over him, and he at once knew why.

"I know where they're at!" exclaimed Julio, opening his eyes and jumping up off the porch.

Rafa stopped playing, "Then, we don't go that way." he said, simply.

"What was that?" Julio shouted, excited, "How did you do that?" he wanted to know.

"The language of the drum speaks in many ways. Learn it and it will show you everything you need to know," said Rafa. He stood from behind the drums. "But first, we need to get the skin."

Julio noticed that Rafa suddenly looked so tired and frail. What had just happened was a miracle to Julio, but at that moment he also understood that the miracle had come at a price. Rafa had taken him on a trip, and the burden was not light.

Julio quickly came over and helped Rafa to the porch where he slowly settled himself into the hammock for a rest. Julio found that he cared much for the old man, and for a moment he thought it might be best to leave so that harm would not come to Rafa.

"In a moment, we go, ya," said Rafa.

Julio went inside the casita. He put on his disguise, changing his shirt for another equally worn and weathered nondescript work shirt. The shoes were beaten, but still comfortable. He'd almost forgotten their original splendor; the way they drew attention and set him apart from any and all in the neighborhood. He recalled the great fight in the subway station and how far gone that life was; a life he'd lived only weeks before. For now he accepted a simple fact; the shoes were just comfortable, nothing more, nothing less. They still had a lot of life left in them; this was obvious, even though they looked like hell.

The fact that Santos and his men hadn't caught him yet was a testament to his ability to slip the streets unnoticed. Still, Julio wondered how much the old man had helped him avoid trouble with his magical drumming. Julio now had no doubt that Rafa's drumming was something out of this world.

Julio looked for the money from where he had kept it, but there was precious little left, only twenty dollars. Julio hoped that would be enough for the skin, and his mind came again to the gun and the two-hundred dollars it had cost him. He cursed himself for spending the money, money he could have used to buy the skin and help Rafa further with food or whatever.

When Julio emerged from the casita, Rafa was asleep. Julio touched his hand and felt the callousness of the fingers, hardened by the endless drumming. In some way, Julio now perceived the hands as those of a magician or a powerful wizard. He'd heard stories like that when listening to the elders in the neighborhood, stories they told about the history of his people back in Puerto Rico. Julio wondered why a man like Rafa, so powerful and wise, would choose to live in the garden as a bum might. He wondered what he would do if he learned the same powers. Would he be so humble? Or, would he seek power and riches, as he knew at times he wanted more than anything?

In his sleep Rafa pulled his hand back, folding it with the other across his chest. He looked so peaceful asleep. Julio sat and waited for him to awake. While he waited, he thought of the language of the drum and what he might learn about himself once he understood its tongue.

CHAPTER 21

Julio found the path and taking it wound his way around the back of the buildings, choosing at random his way to the street. Rafa followed close behind stepping in silence, patiently allowing the boy to pick and choose his way. When they came out, they turned abruptly and walked quickly; giving wide berth to the place they knew Santos and Oscar would be. The old man led the way after a while, but both walked side by side, as father and son might.

As they walked, Julio looked skyward. The day was covered with stormy and uncertain clouds that held tight to the ground as they rolled and rumbled by. The rain had yet to fall, but it looked as if with the slightest provocation the skies would open up and unleash their full fury.

When they reached El Congo Real, it was exactly as Julio remembered it from the few occasions he'd passed by. There were fragile old men and dusty old women, with their spines turned earthward, waiting in soiled plastic chairs that looked as if they themselves might at any moment fall to pieces, tumbling the near broken bodies of the old Hispanic people to the ground.

Julio looked at the people. They looked hopeless and forlorn, until he approached and they smiled and he could see clearly the youthful vigor and playfulness in their eyes. They were still children at heart—that much was clear to see.

Everyone to an individual knew Rafa by name, as he knew theirs, and upon arriving, he went one by one shaking hands with the men and giving out kisses on the cheeks of the ladies, and for each individual he offered a special greeting and a heartfelt hello.

Julio was aware of the love and respect between Rafa and the people who waited patiently on the white plastic chairs. They were all so simple and so happy, or so it seemed to him.

When the Curandero came out he immediately went to Rafa and took up his hand in his.

"Que bueno verte por aqui, Jibaro, siempre es bueno ver al maestro," he said.

Julio's Spanish was weak, but it didn't matter. The admiration and respect shown on the face of the Curandero was obvious when he addressed Rafa.

"Pero el maestro eres tú, Jibaro. Soy un hombre simple y pobre, no soy nada especial como tú," said Rafa, and Julio could see the same love and admiration in Rafa's eyes for the Curandero.

They smiled at each other. Then, Rafa turned to Julio and with a nod waved him near. Julio came, the hat held down, instinctively lowered in his hands.

Rafa switched to English, so that Julio may understand better.

"This is Julio, he wants a skin for his new drum. It's a Boku."

The Curandero was impressed.

"A Boku? Really? What's a young man like you doing with a Boku?" asked the Curandero.

"I built it myself. I want to learn the language of the drum," said Julio.

The Curandero nodded, and looking up to Rafa smiled.

"The Boku is a serious drum," said the Curandero, "You will need to make a sacrifice."

"I heard," said Julio nervously.

Without looking at Rafa, the Curandero said, "Your teacher will show you what to do when the time comes."

The Curandero indicated for Julio to follow him, and back they walked through La Botánica, past the miniature statues of various deities and the medicinal plants, and back further still beyond the racks and stacks of small, dark brown bottles filled with various perfumes and potions, with all their secret powers held tight in the ready by crudely carved corks that jammed the thin necks, each and every label hand written by the wobbly hand of the old Curandero.

They continued back, Julio behind the Curandero and Rafa behind them both, weaving their way past the wares of La Botánica, diving deeper and deeper into the strange spiritual world of Julio's ancestors. Near the back, in the darkest shadows of the shop, the smells were powerfully strong, and in the air Julio felt the presence of things unknown.

They came finally to a large, flat old box on a high table where the Curandero stopped. He opened it and pulled from it a single sheet of what looked like thick paper, except it was very large and looked strikingly similar to the body of flattened hairless goat.

The Curandero held it up to Rafa and after a moment's consideration Rafa nodded. The Curandero, using the top of the box from which it came, rolled the skin into a ordinary looking roll. He produced a rubber band from his pocket and secured the skin for safe travel.

Then the Curandero walked over to a special shelf that held only a few bottles. They seemed different from the rest, perhaps less used, perhaps more special. They were certainly out of the public eye; that much was true. The Curandero carefully selected a bottle and brought it to Rafa who put it in his pocket. Then the Curandero, stopping at another table, brought a small bag that looked to contain some dry leaves. These also were given to Rafa, and they were put into his pocket alongside the small bottle.

Then Rafa nodded to Julio. Julio hesitated, suddenly embarrassed. He dug deep into his pocket to produce the twenty dollars, and then folded it meekly through his fingers. It was all that was left of his remaining money. Finally, he handed it to the Curandero.

The Curandero held it in his open hand for a moment.

"That's it?"

"That's all I got right now, but I can pay more later—if I have to," said Julio, his only relief the fact that it was dark in the back of the shop so that nobody could see him blushing.

Rafa, without hesitation, went into his pocket and produced another twenty, which he handed to the Curandero.

"Here," he said, "the boy will pay me back when he can."

The Curandero nodded, and closed his hand on the money, content with this arrangement.

Julio was silent. He knew this was a lot of money for Rafa, but there was nothing he could do now that would make things better for him.

The three walked in silence out towards the dim light coming through the front of the shop. At the doorway, Julio looked up into the sky and noted the dark bulges that hung heavy from the low cloud cover. He listened to the unease of the rustling treetops in the breeze and in the distance he heard the rumbling of nearing thunder.

Rafa and the Curandero embraced as brothers before departing on long and separate journeys. The Curandero shook hands with Julio and when he did held the hand a moment longer than would be expected.

"The Boku is a powerful instrument, mijo," he offered, "Respect her, and she will teach you everything," he said. "Disrespect her, and she will discipline you with the scorn of a hundred mothers."

Then he let go of Julio's hand and patted him on the back.

Without another look or care, Rafa and Julio left, moving quickly to make the garden before the coming rains with Julio carrying the goat skin behind Rafa's hurried stride. He wondered what the sacrifice would be and what it would mean, and worried about ever disrespecting the drum he was about to complete. The idea of a hundred mothers simultaneously cracking the whip of discipline across his back made his stomach tight with anxiety. He couldn't even handle the scorn of his aunt, and his own mother's scorn was legendary, even more intense than Sylvia's.

With the coming of the dark clouds he felt the coming of a responsibility he may not have the strength to uphold. For the first time, he thought about forgetting this whole drum idea, feeling that the stakes might just be too high for him.

CHAPTER 22

The thunder rolled in unrelenting, coming down with the gathering intensity of a grand summer storm. Before he felt anything, Julio heard the rain connecting with the tops of the garden's trees as the first wayward drops flew in wild and unaccompanied on the outer whippings of earthbound winds.

And Julio was worried.

Julio felt as if he were about to pass a point of no return, into a world where responsibility and expectation would take hold and the flustered failings of his youth would no longer be tolerated by the hundred mothers, or Rafa, or whoever had anything to do with this strange culture of the drum with all its old Puerto Rican souls and fragrant shops and the lines, the hundreds of lines of ancestral expectation. How could anyone expect so much of him when in reality everything he'd ever touched had been ripped to pieces by violence unadorned? Did he want such responsibility? Wasn't it easier to continue to fall short, thereby eliminating any and all expectation? The new questions that surfaced in his mind made him think of what he knew. And for Julio, the streets had long been home.

On the street, personal pleasures ruled the day. To Julio's credit, he'd amassed quite a few already. But he wasn't a true player. Not yet. True players were legendary. Their names permeated the iconic airwaves block by block until whole neighborhoods knew them, feared them, and revered them. By their nature they divided the masses, demanding all to join them, or condemning those who refused to die by the wayside. Their stories were punctuated by an exceptional array of fast living, cash riches, willing women, and blood-set bonds that on a whim could be cemented or broken. A true player ignored the inevitability of endings in favor of the fruit of the moment—a fruit that ripened on the branches of unending, intensely violent confrontations from which one could never back down, no matter how small or seemingly insignificant. On the street, life was a one-way journey flying towards a fireball finish, and in the labyrinth of inevitable endings, one more tragic than the next, a single, simple refrain drove the entire mass barreling forward—at all cost you must eat, or you will be eaten.

Julio knew this world and knew it well. It was a path that was expected of him by many in the neighborhood and beyond, and somewhere, somehow, perhaps simply by virtue of their wishes, it had become a path he had walked and a path he could easily visualize himself taking to its inevitable end. Yet, in his heart of hearts he always knew—it was not his true path, not his true destiny. But he also knew if it came down to it, by the strength of his will alone, he could walk it and walk it well. The drum and its requisite ritual, complete with the realities of coming responsibility, were more intimidating to Julio than any street test had ever been.

The funny thing was for this fact alone Julio stayed—because he refused to come off as a coward in Rafa's eyes. He stayed for the simple reason that he now stood before the watchful eyes of an old man he had grown to love.

Rafa helped Julio lay out the skin in a shallow pan made from the cut bottom of a large old steel barrel. The skin was larger than the edges of the pan itself, a fact that worried Julio, but Rafa seemed unconcerned and so Julio tried his best to ignore the sight. Rafa told Julio to take the large pot off the stove, where it had been placed to heat some water. Julio poured the now warm water into the pan over the goatskin until it lay submerged. Julio stepped back, half expecting the skin to start smoking and sprouting ghost bodies. But it didn't. Instead, only the rain fell with more frequency.

They waited. Rather, Rafa waited while Julio drove himself crazy trying to contain the questions about the sacrifice and what was to come. Rafa was mostly silent, speaking only a few words at the precise moments necessary to instruct Julio in the next step in the process. There was no good moment for questions, but plenty of time to wonder.

After the skin had soaked and softened, Julio removed it from the pan. With Rafa's help, the skin was put onto the drum using the rings that formed the familiar round shape, then the ropes were wound carefully, and the excess skin cut neatly with an old pair of scissors until the drum finally took the completed form.

When the drum was done, Rafa took out the thin scarf printed with the Puerto Rican flag and tied it carefully to cover the head of the drum.

"Can I play it now?" asked Julio.

"No, the skin must be dried. Now is the time for your sacrifice," said Rafa.

Julio swallowed, but the lump in his throat didn't go anywhere.

Lightning lit the darkened sky and the thunder rumbled down like the beating of a thousand booming drums. The rain began to fall in earnest. Rafa produced the small bottle and the satchel of plant matter. He laid both before Julio on the porch.

"Take these," he said, "the liquid is rum made by hand from the cane of a sacred field in Puerto Rico. Under that field lie the bodies of your ancestors. It was an ancient burial ground before it became a cane field." Again the lightning came, this time the crack of thunder followed right on its heels, cutting the sky with jagged edges.

"And this," said Rafa, "These are grasses on which that goat feasted. By these grasses he nourished himself in his life. They also come from Puerto Rico."

Julio was scared. The wind was blowing now with the heavy force of heavens stirred and thunder boomed in every corner of the darkened sky.

"Take these things into the garden," said Rafa, "spread the grass and pour the rum—but only when it is time. Only after you have made a promise to the elders."

Julio's hair flew wild in the wind as a chill shot down his spine.

"What promise?" he asked.

"Is a decision I cannot make for you," said Rafa, simply, "You must decide," and the sky above exploded with thunder and lightning.

Julio took the small bottle and the grasses in his hand. He looked to Rafa and there was no smile on his face. Only the stern, patience and steady eyes, and in them Julio sensed the seeds of gathering expectation.

He wanted to run away. More than anything he wanted to run.

Rafa stood with wind whipping around him, lifting the corners of his jacket and tussling his hair, but Rafa himself stood steady as a statue.

"Go now," he said.

"In the rain?" protested Julio.

"Now is the time," said Rafa.

Julio had no choice. He stepped from the porch and the rain immediately hit him from every angle and not even the sudden assault of the driving rain could distract Julio from Rafa's gaze. When he knelt down, he kept his back to Rafa and the drum, but their presence was impossible for him to ignore.

Julio didn't want to be there in the rain with some silly potions or rum or whatever the Hell he held in his hands so he thought of just tossing their contents down and returning to the porch without another thought. He pulled the cork and was about to do so, when suddenly he thought of his mother. He could see her eyes, her beautiful brown eyes and her gentle temperament towards him. He felt himself, as he'd felt in his infancy, taken up in her caring arms. For the first time in many years, he sensed her in all her motherly glory, and before he knew it, tears welled up in his eyes. He felt the need to honor her and understood that by disrespecting Rafa's instructions he would be disrespecting his own mother, and more than that, her mother, and her mother's mother, and beyond. He felt the weight of his family and his very real responsibility as a part of it.

Tears poured from his eyes and he began to sob just as the rain came down with renewed torrential force. The sky blazed bright white with lightning so close the instant it flashed the sky ripped wide open in a deafening explosion.

Julio made a promise to his mother in that moment, huddled as he was in the bowels of Rafa's garden with the rain pouring off his head, washing his tears from his face down into the soil. He promised his mother that he would make her proud and that he would abandon the streets for a life of promise and responsibility. He poured the rum into the soil that had so willingly taken his tears and the rain and he sprinkled the grasses above all and thanked them for nourishing the goat that would become the voice of his new drum and with the last of the rum he called to the ancestors to bring him wisdom and to teach him the language of the drum.

Then he stood and without wiping his eyes returned to the cover of the porch and Rafa, and finally to stand alongside his very own drum.

CHAPTER 23

The night was spent drying out. A small fire of simple sticks burned on the porch, held in check by the same pan used to wet the skin. Before its humble heat, Julio's wet clothes lay as did the newly dressed drum with the skin basking and drying alongside.

Julio felt as if a huge weight had been lifted from his shoulders. He felt light there on the porch in the setting sun, which had come to set its own evening fire on the horizon after the passing of the rains.

A story occurred to Rafa, one he hadn't told in a long time, and so he told it to Julio. It was a simple story about a fisherman in old Puerto Rico.

"In a fishing village just outside old San Juan, when San Juan was a place to be, a man lived there," began Rafa. "He was a simple man, very simple. Had one boat, a shack near the sand where he lived with his wife and his one son. Alongside in the same way lived his friends, the other fisherman. He was a simple man in an old village. He come home from fishing, sell a few fish to make money for a drink, maybe some dominos too, he play guitar in the afternoon, looking at the sea, his wife in the shack making the good food with good smells coming out. One day, an American man came in a suit and they talk, next day the fisherman take the American out fishing. They go into the sea and the American man catches many fish. He has the best day of his life. For the fisherman, it's a normal day, but for the American, the best day. Ever. They go back and the man sits with his guitar, just like before, just like every day and the American says, 'this place is amazing! There is so much potential here. You know, you should buy some more boats, you can use credit at the bank, you buy the boats and pay your friends some money to take people out fishing. You could make a lot of money, pretty soon you could have ten boats. You can pay some people to cut fish on the shore and prepare lunches, you'd make money there too. In a few years, with hard work, you pay off all the loans and you will have much money, so much you can retire a rich man in just ten years.' This is what the American tells him, all excited, jumping around the old man and his guitar. The fisherman stops playing, and he looks at the American man, 'retire? What do I do when I retire?' asks the fisherman. The American looks at him like he crazy, 'whatever you want' he says, and the fisherman smiles, 'I already do that, pana, everyday,' he says."

CHAPTER 24

The following morning Julio awoke as a child on Christmas morning would. He was in fact, up before Rafa—a first. Rafa made breakfast as he always did as Julio jumped around anxious to tune the drum so that he may begin playing.

After eating, Rafa taught him to tune the drum by pulling on the many ropes and tying the knots one by one, gradually increasing the collective tension on the skin. After only a half hour or so the drum was ready to play.

"So, teach me the language of the drum," said Julio, beside himself with excitement.

Rafa laughed, he laughed long and loud, far longer than Julio felt comfortable listening to.

"What's so funny?!" said Julio, when Rafa finally calmed.

"I'm a simple old man, *no se nada*! I'll teach you how to hit the drum so you don't hurt your hands. But the language of the drum, *mijo*, you must learn that from the drum."

Julio sank down, faced with yet another challenge with no clear path home.

"How will the drum teach me?" he asked.

"Learn to listen, she has much to say."

Rafa came up and in a few moments taught Julio how to hit the drum with the fingers of his open palm on the rim, producing a high almost metallic sound, then he taught him to use all the hand to create an explosive slap nearer the middle of the drum and finally he taught him how to openly strike the middle, a method that created deep rumbling bass.

Julio's new drum sounded good.

"With these three sounds, the drum will begin to speak. You will learn more as you go. All you have to do is listen. Play, and listen," said Rafa.

And then he left to the subway as he did every morning to play for the coins and small bills that would pay for the next day's meal.

Julio, left behind as he'd been almost every day, hidden from the dangers of Santos by the garden, for the first time felt the real accomplishment from the building of the drum. Alone, he rolled the drum across his lap and memorized every color and shape of its shell. He thought again of his promise to his mother and basked in the pride of both his promise and the physical realities of his own drum.

After a while he practiced the strikes that Rafa had taught him and was even able to build up a couple rhythms that he thought were something.

When Rafa returned, Julio had something to show for his day and this made Julio and Rafa both proud.

"Let's play together, sometimes that is a good way to learn," said Rafa, and so they began to play.

Julio had some trouble finding his place within the rhythms Rafa played. It was as if he'd learned nothing real on his own. He was beginning to feel as if he'd wasted his time on all this when all of a sudden he hit a groove and fell right into step with what Rafa was doing.

The rhythm was a good slow groove. Julio held to his path as Rafa danced around him, creating a rich world of sound. Julio saw that Rafa had his eyes closed, so Julio closed his too.

This was better. Julio began to feel the rhythm and gradually lost the apprehension and anxiety that had been blocking him. He began to walk more freely in the landscape of their combined rhythms. He relaxed further and further until again he felt himself floating and flying across the waves of sound. It felt good.

Then, like a shock of cold water thrown from a bucket, Julio had a vision of his aunt, bloodied and crying, dragging her legs across the kitchen floor. The vision was graphic, horribly clear, and laden with sorrow.

He stopped at once and stood.

"What was that?" he demanded.

Rafa slowed, and then also stopped. By his look, Julio knew that Rafa had seen it too. Perhaps with even more clarity, perhaps before Julio himself had.

"What has come, has gone. Is over. Nothing you can do."

But Julio wouldn't accept that.

"What has come? What are you talking about?!" he demanded. He stood, defiant, with the shadows of rage building on the seas of a violent storm.

"There is nothing you can do, mijo. You have seen a possibility of what has recently passed."

Julio waited a moment, then without the hat, without the shirt, without any form of cover or camouflage he ran full steam out of the garden.

Rafa yelled for Julio to come back, but it was too late. The boy was gone.

Rafa wondered at what he'd seen. He hadn't expected Julio to have seen it also. Rafa hadn't even extended his consciousness outside of the garden when the image came. He'd seen Oscar there too, behind Sylvia, with two others; that much he was sure Julio had missed.

Julio ran as he'd never run before, and as he ran the people who saw him were as surprised to see him in the neighborhood as they were to see him run so fast on the broken shoes. By the time he reached his aunt's building, his lungs were burning.

A small crowd clotted the entryway with some on their toes and still others shaking their heads. A man was yelling complaints about the delayed arrival of the police as an ambulance with lights ablaze waited with doors closed below. Julio didn't slow down. He blew through the crowd, flying past the door and beyond their cries and driving his legs up the stairway came around the corner then down the hallway and into the already open door of his aunt's apartment.

Sylvia was on the stretcher, her face beaten and bloodied as it had been in his vision. A paramedic knelt beside her, tending to her wounds. Julio fell to his knees beside her. The whole scene had Santos written all over it. Julio didn't have to see it in his vision because he knew who had done what.

When Sylvia saw Julio her eyes turned and ran but there was nowhere to go and so she began to cry.

"They took my baby, Julio," she wailed.

Julio tried to believe that it wasn't true, that the tragedy before him was all there was. He tried to fathom what she'd just said.

"What? What are you talking about?" was all he could say.

Her tears were coming strong now through her halted breath. The pain of her body was nothing compared to the pain in her heart.

"My baby, they took my baby," she cried and the tears came with heavy, heavy sobs.

Julio looked up and only then saw his two younger cousins. In their faces he perceived the terror they'd just witnessed as their minds also reeled in a sea of unsavory images.

The boy, seeing Julio spoke, "They were looking for you, but she wouldn't tell them anything, then they took Mariela," he said.

The paramedic leaned in, trying to settle Sylvia. She was becoming hysterical.

"Hey kid, you gotta get out of here. She's too upset for this right now. You're making it worse," he said.

Julio wanted to kill him, but the man kept his cool.

"Look, just go downstairs and wait. You can ride in the ambulance to the hospital," he offered.

Julio stood and walked out, stopping once to look back on his aunt Sylvia who lay battered and bloodied on the floor of her kitchen. Then he went downstairs and without a second's pause walked past the crowd, past their cries, past the ambulance, and finally into the lengthening shadows of the coming night.

CHAPTER 25

Julio came back into the garden with purposeful strides. Rafa stood before him, blocking the way into the casita.

"No Julio, you go there, they kill you."

"Get out of my way, old man" said Julio. The veins on his neck were bulging wild, his eyes empty of reason and filled with the rage and hate of revenge.

Rafa knew there was little room for error. He knew that Julio's head was near full now with the shadows of rage and hate and he knew that any words that might stop him from certain death must find their way past his head to Julio's heart.

"Slow down, mijo. Is a trap."

"Don't make me hurt you, Rafa. Get out of my way!"

Rafa stood his ground, "Take a breath, mijo. Think about it."

"I said, get out of my way!"

"They'll kill you!"

Julio jumped forward feigning one way and Rafa, slower in his old wise way, was not wise enough to hold steady and instead found his balance compromised, and with a simple shove Julio put Rafa on the ground. He landed with a crumpling thud on the thin boards of the porch.

Julio didn't even look back. He ripped the carpet from the floor and the trap door flew open, blowing free of the hinges that once held it. Julio knelt and took up the gun. The weight of it calmed him momentarily. Power radiated from the cold hard steel, filling Julio with a sense of righteousness. As if by settling the score, he would find his manhood. He popped open the chamber of the .38 revolver, each of the six chambers held a bullet. He spun it to hear its rattle-snake charm then clapped the chamber shut and slipped the gun into the small of his back.

He turned and behind him stood Rafa, again in the doorway, again defiant, but this time he knew words were no match for Julio's rage.

"I won't let you," he said.

"Then you'll die," Said Julio, and he reached back for the gun.

Rafa knew that this was his only moment, his only chance to stop Julio. But he was old. Perhaps in his youth, perhaps only a few years before, but now—now he didn't stand a chance.

Julio found the gun in the same moment Rafa found his decision. With arms raised and hands grasping, Rafa came at him, lurching for the gun at the end of a clumsy dive. Julio, with practiced ease, stepped back, and raising the gun out of the way, watched as Rafa came full force, focused only on the weapon. As Rafa fell short, his hands scrambled for the pistol, closing on nothing. Julio let him come, until just the right moment, then he swung with cold hard precision, bringing the butt of the gun down onto the back of Rafa's head with a crushing blow.

Crack!

Rafa felt himself loosing consciousness and could only watch as the floor came up at a terrible speed. Unable to adjust, he crashed violently to the ground cutting open the fragile skin of his cheek. Dazed by the blow, Rafa managed to roll on his side and through tormented eyes watched as Julio disappeared beyond the edges of the open doorway of the casita.

Rafa tried to rise, but his balance was gone, so he lay back, flat on his back, and waited for his head to clear.

Julio slipped the gun back, tucking it neatly in the small of his back. Then he took his rage to the streets. He knew that Santos would be at the barbershop. He knew he would be there with his crew and he knew that they would kill him. But, that didn't matter anymore. He was going to take as many of them with him as he could. They had violated his aunt's house—his family, and there was no way to let that go.

The promises of the day before were gone, completely covered by the need for revenge. There was no way to let this go. There was no way Julio could see his way clear to walk away. No choice remained in his mind except to get his cousin back and exact revenge, which meant he'd kill Santos, Oscar, Tony and whoever else it took.

Julio moved silent and undetected through the now dark streets as his initial uncontrolled rage hardened into assassin like resolve. Focused on his simple yet horrific goal, he became a deadly force, with the mind clear of questions, free of the chatter of discussion, unburdened by right and wrong, he knew at that moment the absolute clarity of singular thought and from its seeds the path became crystal clear. Knowing his only hope was to utilize the element of surprise he became also the shadow of a ghost, holding death at the ready in his hands.

Rafa pulled himself up off the floor and stood supported by a hand on the doorway. Julio had bested him, there was nothing more to say. He should have thrown the gun away, he thought to himself. But there was no way to know that Julio would lose control like that. No way to know that his magic would not work on him.

Perhaps he had been wrong about Julio, thought Rafa. Perhaps he was too far gone, too deep in the streets to be saved. The greed had a hold of him with its long pointed nails. Revenge. Hate. Fear. Need. Julio held them so close, so that now it was hard for Rafa to even recognize the Julio he thought he once knew.

He could feel the wound on his cheek dripping blood and with nearly regained balance, felt for the burgeoning lump with his hand that seemed momentarily would become larger even than the rest of his head. It needed ice, but he didn't feel up to getting it now.

Instead, Rafa came to the porch and found a seat on the old rickety chair. It complained heartily when Rafa pushed his weight back, leaning up against the casita wall. He felt the blood still streaming down his cheek and for the moment let it run. There, on the porch, lit by the only light around, sat Julio's drum. Rafa looked over at the drum Julio had built with his assistance. He saw the beauty of it in the overwhelming evidence of intuitive craftsmanship. He saw himself in the fingerprints of Julio's work on the drum. This was the work of a true soul, not a senseless street killer. He'd been right about Julio all along. He knew this, and he wasn't about to let Julio throw it all away.

Rafa knew Julio would run to the barbershop. It was too far for Rafa to make it in time. He'd never catch up to Julio. No matter, thought Rafa, then he walked over to his drums.

Julio came catlike to the front of the barbershop. Inside, it was quiet, too quiet for him. Julio worked his way around back, into the alleyway behind the barbershop until finally he stood before the back door, alone and unafraid.

He tried the door and it was unlocked. Santos had slipped. For the last time, thought Julio, and then he eased his way into the building through the back door.

Rafa, behind his drums, forwent any warm-up and instead began strait away, pounding out a heartbeat like blast on the drums that sent scrambling a pair of small cats that were hiding in the garden bushes. The bass rolled like thunder on the horizon and the skins popped like cracking bats with the slap of his hands. The rhythm was immediately alive and rolling like the waves of a steaming ship through heavy seas. They took to the air, driving in all directions with tremendous force.

Unaware of Rafa's rhythms, Julio steadied himself. He thought he could hear Santos talking on the phone. Julio eased his way quietly through the storeroom, past the stacked shampoo and gel and buckets and the rest. The light of the main floor came in through the cracks of the single curtain, the only thing that separated Julio from Santos. Julio took a deep breath, checked his weapon and jumped through the curtain and out onto the floor.

In the bright light of the shop, Santos stood next to Tony. Before either one could react, Julio had his gun in their faces.

"Why'd you have to do that?!" Julio shouted.

Santos was cool. "Hold up. Let me call you back."

Santos hung up the phone.

Tony went for his gun, but Julio had him beat easy.

"Move and you die!" screamed Julio, and Tony froze cold.

"Cool it, kid," said Santos, real smooth.

"Tell me to cool it again," screamed Julio, pointing the gun at Santos.

Santos just shook his head.

"Give me your guns!" Julio demanded. He was trying to keep calm, but his heart was going a hundred and his lips were shaking.

Tony took out his gun real slow and tossed it onto the counter.

Julio pointed down Santos.

Santos scoffed.

"Kid, if I had my gun on me, you'd be dead."

"Shut up!" screamed Julio, "Tell me where my cousin is!"

Rafa's hands blurred above the drums as the rhythms rumbled from the skins. His head erect and his eyes on distant lines, Rafa played with all his heart. In a moment he sensed the danger at the barbershop and so played with more intensity clarifying the scene. He could see by way of understanding and energy, Julio surrounded by the shadows of Santos and Tony. Treachery clouded the air with choking thickness. Julio was in great danger and so Rafa played to bring himself into the barbershop itself. He played to manifest somehow, to cross over with his energies so that he might help the boy. He played with everything he had.

Tony was nervous as he kept eyeing his gun, then Julio, then Santos. His eyes were wild with what to do next. Santos was nervous too. That is, until he got a good look at Julio's gun, then he suddenly became cool. Too cool. Santos sat back on the edge of the counter and he folded his arms.

"You got that gun from Fast Eddie," he wasn't asking.

"What?" said Julio, pointing the gun even more nervously at Santos.

"Well," said Santos, "me and Fast Eddie, we go way back." He smiled.

Tony shuffled around, more nervous than ever.

"In fact," added Santos, "if he ever sold a gun to a kid like you who might be buying it to come kill me," Santos shook his head, "well, let's just say he knows better."

"Just tell me where my cousin is at!" demanded Julio, trying his best to hold on to the situation, but he could tell that Santos had something big up his sleeve.

Santos stood and began to walk casually in front of Julio.

"I don't think Fast Eddie would do that, do you Tony?" but Tony was too scared to answer.

"No," said Santos, "I don't think he would. You know why? Because if that kid misses, and I survive, he dies. And you too, kid. You die, too."

Santos was making up his mind, and a moment later he did.

"You know what?" he said, "Tell you what I'm gonna do. I'm gonna get my gun, and I'm gonna shoot you dead. You can try and shoot me, but you better not miss."

And Santos started to do just that, walking with collected precision towards his hanging jacket.

"STOP!" shouted Julio, "Just tell me where she is!" he demanded.

Santos held up for a moment, he shook his head.

"Kid, I don't know what you're talking about. I have no idea where she is," he said, then he thought a moment, "you should have tried the library."

Santos went for his gun.

Julio aimed careful, right in the center of Santo's chest, then he pulled the trigger and couldn't help close his eyes for the thunderous explosion that would come complete with belching flame and lurching bodies.

But there was only a flat empty click that didn't even echo in the warmth of the well used barber shop. He pulled the trigger again, and again, and nothing.

Sweat poured from Rafa's head as he played. He sensed the desperation in Julio at once and the assured victory in Santos. The shadows became so dark that Julio was no more than a speck of light in the darkest night. He played, hoping to bring his powers to the boy, but the darkness of Santos overwhelmed him. Regardless, Rafa played on.

Santos reached his hanging jacket and pulled out his own weapon, a platinum plated 9mm automatic, he took time to cock it and ensure it was loaded. With the same casual fare, Santos walked over to Tony's gun as it lay on the counter, he picked it up and held it a second, "Here," he said, tossing it to Tony. When Tony caught it, he shook his head in relief.

"By the way," Santos said, "you're worthless." Then he shot Tony in the gut.

Tony doubled over in complete shock, stumbling back, blood pouring from the wound through his helplessly clutched fingers. When Tony struggled to raise his own gun to shoot, Santos put two more into him, blowing him back against the far wall.

Santos pointed the weapon at Tony as he spoke to Julio, "You see, he should have shot you when you came in. What's the point of a body guard that can't guard nobody?" he said.

Julio frantically went at the .38 fighting for reason and understanding. Desperate, he opened the chamber and only then realized after pulling the trigger once more than the gun had no firing pin. It would not shoot. Ever.

"Fast Eddie has a couple of those," said Santos. He smiled, "You think you're the first person to think of buying a gun and killing me?" he asked, and then he laughed out loud.

Julio remembered Fast Eddie. He remembered him showing fear when he pointed the gun at him. He remembered knowing inside that Fast Eddie had recognized him, and he remembered ignoring that fact. Fast Eddie had tricked him and tricked him good. Julio felt foolish, and then dropped the useless gun to the ground. His only hope was pleading for his life; a play he knew would bring him a few seconds more, perhaps less.

"Now this gun," said Santos, indicating the gun he held, "this gun is the gun you used to kill Tony." He held his weapon to one side and walking over to Tony's dead body, with the other hand picked up his discarded weapon. "And this one," he said, holding Tony's unused gun, "is the one he used to kill you."

Julio began backing up.

"Nice and clean, no?" said Santos, checking Tony's weapon quickly.

Rafa brought the sum of his playing to the barber shop. In a great crescendo that brought people to newly lit windows, people who had heard Rafa play many, many times before, people who for the first time in their lives heard drumming so frantic, so intense, so suddenly urgent, Rafa played like never before.

They came to their lit windows and looked down on the shadows of the garden where the only sound—an intense wall of rhythmic desperation—rose in all directions like the flames of a giant out of control fire. They came to see what was happening, and what was happening was Rafa's body powerfully beating the drums to tinder on the garden grounds while his spirit fought to save the boy who was now as good as dead.

Julio took another step back just as Santos raised his gun to fire. Julio had a glimpse down the barrel of the gun as it aligned itself with his face.

"You dead, kid." Said Santos, but before he could fire that fatal shot, Oscar appeared alone just inside the curtain.

Santos swung the gun around, held it a second, and then in frustration raised his arms up in the air.

"Oh, just in time," said Santos. "Where the hell you been?" he demanded, "This kid almost killed me!"

Oscar smiled then surveyed the scene. Tony lay in a bloody mess against the far wall. Oscar sucked his teeth three times, "tsk, tsk, tsk."

"Yea, sucks to be him," Santos said.

With Oscar there, Santos relaxed a bit, "You been looking for this kid a hot minute, how is it he shows up out of nowhere with a gun?" asked Santos, then he turned to Julio, "Who you think you are anyway? Rob me? You stupid or something?"

Julio was about to say something, he was about to try and get himself out of it when Santos raised the gun to fire. Julio closed his eyes.

The shot went off and Julio instinctively flinched in the instant the sound reached his ears. He waited for the punch and pain of impact, he waited a fraction of a second and nothing came. He opened his eyes to see Santos falling headlong towards his side, the pistol forming a wide arc as his body fell with his arm swinging round, looking to fire at the man who'd just shot him dead with a single bullet to the heart. But the heart quit before the arm got the message, and before Santos had the chance to shoot anyone ever again, he fell dead on the barbershop floor.

His gun popped free, skated the tile floor, and stopped only inches from Julio's feet.

Oscar stood off to the side, where he'd been since coming in, holding a still smoking gun.

Julio's mind went wild. Santos was dead! Oscar had killed Santos with a single shot! A second ago Santos was alive, holding the gun meant to kill him!

Oscar walked with a casual coy stride to the fallen body, as if he were approaching a girl at a dance. He paused over top to examine his handiwork, and for the moment, ignored Julio and the fallen weapon.

As his breath came back, Julio considered the gun and what he'd just seen. He could see the trigger. It seemed to wink at him in the bright barbershop lights. Visions came to his mind. He imagined his hand closing on the grip and taking the gun up. He saw himself doing a quick sideways roll and come up firing. BLAM! BLAM! He saw Oscar falling and saw his rise to power. Then he would become the O.G. of the neighborhood. The vision filled him with a desperate desire.

"Go! Go! Go!" screamed his mind, deafening his senses. His mind told him Oscar would probably kill him anyway. He felt his knees loosen and his fingers go hungry.

Rafa's playing changed instantly. He pulled back, the rhythm jumping track, moving now into a slow island beat with the sun shining and the waves like diamond dusted mounds rolling onto the sand.

He called out with a song, his voice breaking, the tears welling up in his eyes. Gentle melodies lifted out of the garden and the people in the windows felt their own hearts pulled down into the garden. A woman broke out in tears. A man stepped back from the open window, clutching his jaw, frozen by a memory long gone. People all around felt the urge to hug and hold each other. Mothers took up their children in their arms. More than one joined him in the simple song, while others threw down everything and for reasons unknown headed to the garden to find Rafa and his song.

There was only a moment for Julio to get the gun and shoot Oscar. If he could pull off the final kill, he would own the world.

Knowing this he glanced down at the gun. Julio could hear its promise loud and clear. Across the room Oscar leaned in, seemingly unaware, over Santos's fallen body. Julio could feel the beckoning gun, he could feel it calling to him, he could feel the sum of his desires—for power, riches, the girls, the fast cars, parties, and the endless amenities of watches, chains and a closet full of head turning sneakers. He wanted it all, he realized, and now only a single bullet and a quick hand separated him from that dream. He could have it all—all of it. A whole new world lay before him, waiting at his feet.

Without another breath of thought and as quick as he could, Julio went for the gun, his eyes dropping in that final moment to find the pistol grip.

Suddenly, everything fell into slow motion as it had for Julio in the Subway fight. As he reached for the gun, Julio glimpsed Oscar's hand from the corner of his eyes just as it became a blur, like a flash, quick as a light flicking on, quicker than Julio had ever been, and

Julio saw with the clarity of dreaded dismay as Oscar's gun emerged just enough to fire from low off the hip. Even before Julio's hand could close on the gun that waited for him at his feet, the gun came alive with the arrival of Oscar's bullet and blew back between his legs, scattering across the floor until it reached the far wall.

Julio froze. Then with nothing more to do, he straightened up slowly, his empty hands shaking.

Oscar, with his gun poised and a whisper of smoke trailing from the barrel, smiled. The eyes, the ever calm, all seeing eyes of Oscar held onto Julio, held him as giant hands would a struggling insect. Eyes that looked right through Julio. One flinch and Julio knew Oscar would shoot him dead. Oscar raised the gun, passing the point at which a bullet would gun Julio down and continued raising the barrel until it met his lips. Like a cowboy in a western, Oscar blew the smoke from the barrel of the gun and then he smiled.

Suddenly, the back doorway blew open and three men busted in with guns drawn. Julio recognized them immediately. It was the three who had robbed him of the drug money a few weeks back. Julio was sure that the men had come to kill and rob Santos and his gang again. Fear shot through him as he realized he would be killed along with Oscar as one of his gang.

But they didn't do anything. They just came in and held their ground.

"It's cool, clean this up," said Oscar in a deep, calm and sweet voice.

Julio had never heard Oscar speak. Nobody had. Like a snake's might sound, thought Julio, and the three men jumped into action, dragging bodies into position and setting weapons to make it seem as if both men had gunned each other down.

By subtle indication Oscar directed the three and they did exactly as they were told. Content with the progress of the work, Oscar turned his attention away from the men and held Julio again in his gaze.

Rafa was tiring, but he played on, increasing the volume, speeding the rhythms, knowing the danger surrounding Julio. He knew now that Oscar was there, Oscar was easy for him to perceive, and he knew that Santos and Tony were dead. He sensed the great evil of Oscar as it enveloped the space within the barbershop. By comparison, the light of Julio was a distant spec of fading light in a deep dark sky.

In a moment, Rafa feared, he would no longer be able to perceive Julio. He played with all his might to bring light into Julio so that he would not be lost to Oscar's darkness.

Sweat covered the old man, his skin gleaming in the frail light of the moon, his hands a blur, the muscles taught in tenuous ribbons jumping out against the skin, his face straining to maintain the powerful strikes on the drum as the thunderous rhythmic sounds rose like giant crashing waves on all sides. Some of the people from the windows were down with him now in the garden and what they saw made their hair stand on end.

Rafa, his shirt soaked to the skin with sweat, his eyes clamped shut, the blood streaming from the cut on his face, and his hands flying like the legs of a race horse run wild, the palms and fingertips beating with intense precision against the skins of the drum. And the sound! Gigantic tribal rumblings unlike anything anyone had ever heard. The sound was immense, enveloping the night with urgency and drive.

Never before had anyone seen the old man play so hard, never before had anyone seen him so ragged. It looked as if his arms might break off at any moment.

A man with no shirt, fresh from his living room, approached Rafa and yelling over the drums tried in earnest to get him to stop.

"Hey!" he shouted. "Hey, man, you better take a rest, gonna get hurt playing like that!"

But Rafa couldn't hear him. He played on, with his muscles aching and his heart and lungs screaming. He played with everything he had and borrowed what he couldn't come up with from places unknown.

The man without a shirt tried again, and then others joined in. It seemed to them that if Rafa were to continue, he would die of a heart attack right there. The man without a shirt came close and putting his hand on Rafa's shoulder tried to pull him away.

"This man's burning up!" he declared. He could feel the muscles firing under the thin fabric of the shirt like steel wires strained to the limit.

He pulled again, but Rafa would not move. "If he don't stop, he gonna kill himself." the man decided, and others coming forward from the gathering crowd came to help.

The men pulled at Rafa but could not remove him from behind the drums. So they did the next best thing; they started removing drums. They took one out of Rafa's reach, and as if by design he consolidated on the remaining two. They took another, leaving him with the one clutched fiercely between his legs. On this one remaining drum Rafa played, the rhythm now less massive, less booming, yet in some way more focused.

Julio thought about running and Oscar just shook his head and began walking forward with his gun pulled. It was as if Oscar were somehow in his head. Julio suddenly became very scared, more scared than he ever imagined he could be. More scared than he'd ever been, even with Santos pointing a gun at him. Just as it seemed the fear would explode his mind, Julio gave in. He gave up his fear and faced certain death as a decorated warrior might a firing squad. Do what you got to do, he thought, and took one last sweet breath of air.

Suddenly, Julio heard Rafa's playing. It came on quick, as if he'd been deaf before and could now hear. The rhythms were clear and for the first time he felt the old man there with him in the room. He could feel the old man all around, creating a wall of protection from which he knew Oscar could not penetrate. Julio's breath came again and he truly relaxed for the first time in what seemed like lifetimes. He relaxed and allowed Rafa's rhythms to come into him.

Three men were pulling at the drum between Rafa's legs and three men with all their might could not relieve him of the drum. It was now painfully obvious to everyone there that Rafa would play until he died, and at that moment it seemed as if he would be dead any second.

Rafa's eyes were clamped shut and he didn't seem to notice any of the crowd around him. In fact, even as the drums were being taken, he didn't open them, and he didn't miss a beat that whole time.

One of the men pulled at Rafa's arm, trying to get him to stop. The arm kept kicking, the hands beating upon the skin of the drum. He pulled harder, and harder still, until Rafa fell off the stool and lading on his side continued to play the single remaining drum.

"Well, I'll be! Will you look at that!" said one.

"Never seen anything like it," said another.

"What do you think got into him?" asked still one more.

"Man's trying to kill hiself," said the man with no shirt, standing above Rafa holding his hands on his hips.

Oscar could sense the old man in Julio's eyes. He knew the consequences of what was happening. He perceived the weakness of the old man and the newfound serenity of the boy. The boy had served Oscar well; an unwitting accomplice helping him to overthrow Santos and his gang. However, the boy was expendable and always had been. He was a liability now, having seen so much blood. There was no way to trust his mouth or his own greedy desires which might someday compete with Oscar's own.

Oscar wondered about Julio. He knew he should just kill him, but something compelled him to take a closer look. So Oscar looked deep into the soul of the boy. He looked as long as he liked.

After a moment he saw what he was looking for. Or more to the point, he didn't find what he was looking for. He put his gun away.

"Go home," said Oscar. "I'll send your cousin there, she'll be waiting for you."

Julio stood there, unwilling to move. He wasn't afraid anymore and so he watched Oscar's eyes a moment longer. In them he saw a vision of violent death at the hands of the three who were now helping with the takeover of Santos. He saw Oscar's dead body as clearly as he'd seen his aunt's, bloodied on her kitchen floor.

Julio smiled, causing Oscar for the first time in Julio's memory to shift uneasily from one side to the other. Oscar's eyes lit up with rage.

"Go now," said Oscar, regaining his composure, "before I change my mind."

But Julio was already walking out and didn't waste a moment looking back.

Rafa, with the three men again hanging on his arms stopped struggling and suddenly fell disturbingly still.

"Get him onto the porch," one said.

"Somebody call an ambulance!" shouted another.

"This mans plum crazy!" said the man with no shirt.

Julio left the shop and finding the freedom of the night air ran. He ran all the way back to his aunt's house where he found his cousin safe at home hiding behind the locked door, told by Oscar's men that if she moved or made a peep they'd be back to kill them all. She was shaken, but unhurt, and when Julio came to the door she broke out crying, and then tried to slap him, then cried some more and finally the two of them hugged for the first time in many, many years.

They called the hospital and both Julio's other nephews were safe, Sylvia also, steady, recovering as Julio knew she would.

"Go to her," said Julio, "I'll be there soon."

And the oldest cousin left without pause, hurrying to the hospital.

CHAPTER 26

Julio approached the garden with reservation. He had failed to uphold his promise to his mother and above that had felt again the greed and desire for instant power that came with the selling of drugs. That greed and desire more powerful than anything he could control. He knew that if it hadn't been for Rafa, he would have been killed, and knowing this he cowered before the gates of the garden.

Rafa lay in the bed inside the casita, having recovered just in time to stop the coming of the ambulance and having made his way to the bed, convinced the people to leave him alone. All except the man with no shirt who just at this moment was leaving.

As the man passed the gates of the garden on his way out he found Julio waiting outside.

"What you doing out here, boy?" asked the man.

Julio put his hands into his pockets.

"I'm going to see the old man," said Julio.

"Well, that man's crazy! He damn near killed hiself tonight playin them damn drums," said the man.

Julio shrugged his shoulders. There was that too, Rafa must have played like crazy just to reach him all the way off in the barber shop.

"Don't know if you should see him," said the man with no shirt, "he don't look so good, all tired out."

The man looked at Julio, who still didn't say anything.

"Wait till morning, boy, he be better by then," he said, and then the man with no shirt walked away.

Julio waited for him to leave. Then he waited a little bit more, and then he walked into the gates of the garden towards the feeble light burning on the porch of the casita.

He stepped lightly to the front of the casita. From outside he could see across the old tired boards of the porch and into the small one room casita where Rafa lay on the bed, the cut on his face bandaged, his eyes closed and his hands folded by feeble arms across his chest.

Julio remembered their fight. He remembered pulling out the gun and striking Rafa with the butt of it on the back of his head. He remembered the horrible sound it made and he wondered if he would ever stop hurting people who loved him as he knew the old man loved him now. Shame filled Julio's heart as he watched the old man sleep on the little bed, the bed of a poor old man who tried to help him. He couldn't face him, not like this, not after all he'd done to him. Julio turned to go.

"You hard headed," said Rafa from the bed, "just like me." Rafa looked over, a smile on his face and in his eyes.

"I'm sorry I hit you, Rafa. I was crazy mad," said Julio.

"Lucky for me you hit like a girl" said Rafa and both he and the boy laughed a bit.

But, Julio could see how Rafa was playing strong for him now. He could see that in reality Rafa was very tired still, and so Julio walked into the casita and taking the chair sat beside his bed.

"You rest, viejo. Give it time," said Julio, watching over him.

"Si," said Rafa, "I tired." But there was no remorse or blame or any other such worry in his voice. The old man was content, happy in the way things had come to pass. He took a deep breath as Julio sat watching over him.

"Julio," said the old man after a long while, "I want to tell you something."

But Julio was already asleep in the chair, with his head leaned up against the wall.

"You make me proud tonight, mijo, you done good," said Rafa, then he fell quiet too.

CHAPTER 27

Julio awoke with the low strokes of the sun's first rays as they colored with increasing courage the corners of the casita. Light came to his eyes, interrupting a dream he'd been having, of which only the feelings of fear and panic remained, like the sands washed high beyond the flow of an outraged river.

He hadn't meant to fall asleep there, not like that. He looked down at Rafa, who lay motionless on the bed. He knew Rafa would be too tired to play at the subway today and he knew that the old man needed to eat a good breakfast and in searching found no money with which to buy the old man's preferred food.

Then Julio had an idea.

He grabbed his drum and Rafa's old collection hat and the stool and with a concealed smile and the emotion of pending good deeds he headed out with the day's first light towards the Subway.

It was a beautiful day, with the sun shining already bright as it topped the buildings of East Harlem. Julio felt good, and happy to finally have the opportunity to pay the old man back for all his kindness. He couldn't wait to make the money for the food and for once make the old man breakfast. He worried a bit about how bad his drumming would be, but not too much, not enough to cause him to turn around.

At the same place Rafa sat every day, Julio set up the stool and the hat and sat finally before his own hand made drum. The shopkeeper came out and raised his eyebrows, but he didn't say anything, preferring to wait and see. Others on the sidewalk also paused to note Julio's presence there in place of Rafa.

Julio looked around and felt the nerves bubbling in his stomach. He didn't know what he was going to play, but figured a half dozen eggs, a couple plantains and a scoop of rice would cost him about five dollars, and so he said to himself that as soon as he got the five dollars in the hat, he was going to get the Hell out of there.

Just then Coco came up with the big kid from the subway fight. They stood over him a moment, wondering.

"Julio?" said Coco, unsure.

He looked up at her.

The big kid broke out laughing, his broken arm healing, the scar on his face a faded memory.

"Look at your bum ass!" he shouted and pointed with the good hand.

And Julio looked down at himself. He saw the shoes and the simple jeans and tattered shirt and what he saw brought him no shame. Looking up again at Coco and the big kid, both of whom wore designer clothes that undoubtedly far outstripped their financial means, he smiled.

"He's smiling!" said the big kid, "bum ass lost his mind!"

"You done good, Julio, you finally made it!" squealed Coco, beside herself with laughter.

In some way Julio felt that she was right. He'd made it. He'd made some kind of step in a long, beautiful journey. It wasn't in a direction he knew the way, but even with the broken shoes and the old clothes he was happier now than he ever imagined he could be.

Coco and the big kid went off, laughing and looking back at Julio as they walked away. The big kid turned when he was halfway down the block, "Looser!" he shouted. They were acting happy, thought Julio, but they were nowhere near as happy as he was to be there, ready to play his drum so he could help his friend Rafa get a good meal.

He began with some timid strikes, modeled on what he remembered from Rafa's teaching the day before. He played as if not to disturb any of the people walking by on the streets. The shop keeper watched a few moments more of this and shaking his head, walked back inside. People walked by, not even paying

Julio any mind, and the hat remained empty before him.

Julio, presently ignored by the masses, started to relax and with the newly found space in his mind and heart began to explore the drum a bit more. He played with heavier hands, bringing more sound to the drum, finding one rhythm then another. Sweat began to form under his arms and on his forehead as he played, as he ramped up the speed and volume. He loosened his shoulders, back and neck and the speed in his hands picked up even more and the fingers began to dance a bit on the skin with the palms bouncing and dancing and everything, even the air around him, was dancing now.

A few coins fell into the hat and Julio smiled. Then a few more. He kept playing, encouraged by the clink of the coins. The shop keeper even came out and dropped some loose change into the hat and Julio smiled at him too.

The man with no shirt from the night before came up and stood before Julio. He was agitated and stood on restless feet.

"Boy," he finally said, "what the hell you think you doin? You got no sense, boy."

Julio stopped playing, the smile fading from his face.

"What'da mean?" asked Julio.

. "How can you be out here like that on a day like today?"

"I don't understand," said Julio. A small crowd was forming around them.

"Boy, that old man died this morning and you out here drummin like you having a parade."

Julio stood up alarmed.

"What?" he said, "Who died?"

"That ol' drummin fool, that's who!"

"Nobody died! Rafa isn't dead, he was just resting from last night." Julio came around the drum. He came around the drum ready to beat the man down.

But the man with no shirt held steady. "He dead, they takin his body away right now and you's throwin a party."

Julio grabbed his drum and the hat that spilled the coins as he ran full speed back to the garden. His heart was pounding in his chest and eyes burning with what he hoped were just evil lies told by the man. As he ran, he thought about how when he got there and found out the man was lying, he'd go out and look for him and teach him a serious lesson in truth telling. There was no way Rafa was dead, he couldn't die, he thought.

But, as he approached the garden he saw the ambulance. He slowed to a walk. First the hat, then the drum fell from his hands. He got to the garden gate and with a lump like a brick in his throat he forced himself to look in. But it was already over. Rafa was nowhere to be seen. For a moment he let himself believe that Rafa had gotten up and walked away.

But when he turned he saw the open door of the ambulance and the police man and he heard the word "dead" and so he went into the garden and sat against the tree where he'd put down his sacrifice in the rain and he stared at the casita that had been his friend's home. Their home.

There were so many memories and hopes for the future flooding his vision that as he sat there watching, he didn't even notice when a woman brought in the hat and his drum and set them just beyond the shade of the tree, and he didn't notice either when they took Rafa's body away in the ambulance flashing no lights and making no sound.

CHAPTER 28

After the funeral, Julio walked alone into the garden. He closed the gate behind him and walked in. The plants were fully grown now, at least those that would die in the coming of the cold winter months. Already, without Rafa's careful hand, the garden lacked discipline, and so littered the grounds with its leaves and stray blown twigs and such. Julio walked past, remembering the garden when it was also the home of the old man. The whole place seemed so grey, even on this, a beautiful, late summer's day.

Julio pushed open the door to the casita. Inside he found his drum sitting by the bed where Rafa had slept last. He missed the old man very much. In the week that passed between his death and today, Julio had spent each night sleeping on the lonesome porch.

Julio took out the drum for the first time since the death of the old man. He remembered his sacrifice in the rain and the careful, never judgmental direction of the old man. He could still hear his voice, clear as if it were being spoken today.

Julio took the stool and went out to the tree in the garden and started to play. This time he just closed his eyes and with a breath began to beat the drum with an easy touch. He dove into his feelings for the old man and all the sorrow welled up and overtook him. Tears began to fall from his eyes and all the while Julio played and played and played. For a long while he played like this with emotion pouring from him and just when Julio thought it would never stop, it did.

He became acutely aware of the rhythms he was playing. There was something in there, something he was hearing that called to him. He changed the pattern slightly, bringing clarity to what he was hearing. More pronounced, it came off the drum with thunderous precision. Within the sound Julio felt the coming of the old man, Rafa, and he welcomed him in. He played steady, holding the rhythm so that the vision would come clear. At once all the sorrow was gone. The rhythm formed what seemed like a sentence of words, but in a language he could not understand. The rhythm rolled in giant circles finding its way around and around and each time Julio listened, straining for meaning, and each time it rolled by defiantly indifferent. Julio heard the old man laughing in the sound of the drum and he heard in his laughter, or rather felt, the old man say 'you try to hard for everything, let this thing come to you' and so Julio stopped trying to hear the words of the drum, and for the first time just sat back and *felt* the language of the drum in his heart and soul, and suddenly he understood everything.

He understood that the old man died a happy old man with a life of pleasantries tailed out behind him, memories from which, if he wished, Rafa could have pulled a hundred thousand smiles, but memories that he had left, in favor of each and every moment of his life. Moments devoid of regret or expectation and he knew the old man had never held expectations for him and he knew that in this way the old man was never in any way disappointed in Julio. He had only loved him, as a father would, guiding him with the truest of intentions while allowing him to find his own way.

Julio stopped playing. He thought about his road to the tree with the hand built drum between his legs. He looked down at the busted sneakers at his feet and remembered again what they had meant to him at the beginning of the summer. They were still a symbol, he thought, they were the same shoes as before, but now they meant so much more, more than they ever did, more than he ever imagined possible.

He thought about the sneakers and the old man and the drum and he smiled. Under the tree in Rafa's garden, he smiled, and couldn't remember a time in his life when he'd felt so happy and free.

ABOUT THE AUTHOR:

After returning from the Peace Corps (Bolivia), Araby Patch graduated with an MA in English Education from Columbia University's Teacher's College and began teaching GED in the South Bronx and East Harlem. After six wonderful, rewarding years of working with a number of incredibly talented and vibrant New York City young adults, Araby left to pursue his dreams of becoming a writer. *Of Dreams and Drums* is his first published novel.

www.ingramcontent.com/pod-product-compliance
Lightning Source LLC
Chambersburg PA
CBHW051833170626
46807CB00003B/1157